Dedicated to all my fellow Dog Fashion Disco fans
and to the *real* Mushroom Cult.
(You all know who you are.)

And a special dedication to the real-life Hapney,
as she left for the netherworld way before her time.
(Feb 7, 1987 – July 1, 2021)

Editor: Denise Barker
Chapter Artwork: Amy Hunter
Author Photo: Elisabeth B. Adams
1984/1994 Handwriting insert: Ashley Mayer
Front Cover, Back Cover, & Title Page artwork,
and 4 adverts: Kyle Lechner
Formatting: Kari Holloway

Published by Scout Media
www.ScoutMediaBooksMusic.com
Copyright 2021
ISBN: 978-1-7368867-1-7 (print)
ISBN: 978-1-7368867-2-4 (eBook)

April 15, 2021 — July 7, 2021
(Fort Belvior, VA)
For more information on my books & music:
www.BrianPaone.com

1: DAY OF THE DEAD

The Vertigo Motel's flashing sign outside its glass front doors made the vacant lobby pulsate with neon red, then blackness, then neon red, then blackness ... The shadows from the discarded reception desk and the overturned chairs joined in a staccato dance to the beat of the light.

Smith bent over and gripped the back of a toppled chair to set it upright. Dust plumed from underneath the legs when he got it situated. He glanced behind him and noticed his single line of shoeprints embedded in the dust atop the floorboards leading from the front door to where he currently stood. He had no recollection of entering the motel, nor how he had gotten here in the first place.

The faint buzzing from the neon sign made it difficult for him to collect his thoughts and to recall what had happened to him. He coughed, and the sound ricocheted down the barren first-floor hallway. Noise from his own body and not the incessant buzzing from the sign outside jolted his brain into overdrive. He rubbed his palm over the shirt at his chest as he remembered the tightness in his heart he had felt just moments earlier.

"Am I dead?" he asked the empty motel.

A Polaroid photograph drifted downward from somewhere in the ceiling, gliding, like a feather, until it landed half on the toes of his right shoe and half on the dust-blanketed floor. The picture was of him, standing in front of this motel years earlier—an era long forgotten to the stains of time. It resembled the same photograph Eva/*Anya* had given him in his PI office so many years ago of George Covington standing in front of the Vertigo.

Only this time, Smith was in George's spot.

Smith pocketed the Polaroid and noticed a crumpled package of Smolens cigarettes on the reception desk. He grabbed the pack and peered inside; it was filled with bits and pieces of something that may have been the semblance of a cigarette in another lifetime. He threw the package onto the floor and sighed.

A high-pitched scream erupted from behind the first door on the right, and Smith stumbled backward. Then silence. He strained his ears, tilting his face to the left, toward the hallway, and swallowed hard. He scanned the floorboards in front of him leading to the first-floor rooms and realized the dust was devoid of prints, other than his. *No one has walked these floors in decades.*

"Help me!" a woman screamed. "Is someone out there? Please be out there!"

Smith dipped his hand into his pocket to retrieve the Polaroid for another glance before he decided his next move. However, his fingers first grazed something round and hard.

As he removed his hand, a shopworn pocket watch attached to a chain revealed itself. "What in tarnation?" he mumbled. It had been lost forever.

"I can hear you out there! *Please* help me!"

Smith stepped forward, creating a new set of prints in the untouched and age-old dust.

"Please hurry! I think he's dead. I think ... I think he had a heart attack."

Smith halted, gripping his shirt over his chest. His knees buckled, and he collapsed to the floor, sending a wave of dust against the walls. *Is she talking about me? Am I having the heart attack? Wasn't I having a heart attack earlier?*

The image of his granddaughter Melissa jumping from her first-floor bedroom windowsill as the police and his son barged into her bedroom flashed through his mind.

Smith put both palms on the floor and pushed himself upright.

"Are you fucking going to help me? *Hello?*"

"Yes ..." His voice cracked, and he cleared his throat. "I'm coming." Smith shuffled toward the first door in the hallway and tried the knob. It turned with ease, and he swung open the door.

A woman with a gag wrapped around her chin, where she had spit it out, and half-naked in tattered clothes sat against the far wall, chained to the steam heater. One leg was bent underneath her, and the other laid straight forward. She jerked her head from side to side to flit her brown hair from her sweaty face. She raised both arms to highlight the handcuffs. "You got a key to this?"

Smith squinted and peered at her from the corner of his eye. "Who are you?"

"Who are *you*?"

Smith shook his head. "How long have you been here? There are no prints on the—"

"How long have *you* been here?"

"Good gravy, woman. I'm asking the questions here. You're the one tied to a radiator who needs the help."

She scrunched her lips and nodded once in agreement. "I followed my husband here. He was fucking that bitch from the tennis club. She's, like, a freshman in college or something. Works there only on the weekends. College kid, hands out towels to all the yuppies. I *knew* he had a thing for her. And I had suspected he was bringing her here to bang her for quite a while now."

Smith scratched an itch over his right eyebrow as his brain fell right back into his old detective thinking. Some tricks just couldn't be forgotten or ignored. He stepped farther into the motel room. "Do you know where we are?"

"Are you asking because you're confused or because you're trying to see if I'm a nutjob?"

Smith eyed the water-stained ceiling. "Maybe a little of both."

The woman rocked her body left to right to readjust her angle against the radiator. "The Hawthorne."

Smith's eyes flitted from the ceiling to her tear-stained face. "The Hawthorne?"

"Fucking Hawthorne Hotel. In Salem, you dunce."

Smith took a step backward, enough to peek around the doorjamb and survey the hallway. "*Um*, look, doll. This might be hard to swallow, but we're in the Vertigo Motel. In Vegas. But …" He furrowed his brows as he studied the chained woman again. "But that burned down decades ago."

"Either you're smoking the crack pipe or you're senile, old man."

Smith took a handful of quick steps toward her and stopped. "Humor me for a moment. What do you see around you? What does the room look like?"

The woman chortled. "Sure, the hotel is beautiful and a tourist trap, but I think their rates don't match their service. It's certainly pretty to look at. I completely get why he takes her here to fuck her. It impresses her. Mr. Always-One-Step-Ahead can play the bigshot, up-and-coming attorney to the little college girl. I'm sure she just *swoons*"—the woman exaggeratedly batted her eyelashes—"when he pulls up in that new, red T-top IROC of his. So, what are you anyway? Room service or something? You're too old to be a bellhop. Took you long enough to hear me."

"Wait a minute. Always one step ahead? And he drives an IROC?"

"That's what he says his catchphrase will be when he gets his own practice. It's a play on his last name. His is spelled with two *P*s. S-T-E-P-P. So are you gonna get me out of these—"

"Your husband is Attorney Stepp?"

"Ha! If you can call what he does being an attorney. More like a lying, cheating, sad excuse for a lawyer. Now can you please get these off me so I can give him a taste of his own medicine?" She raised her arms and jiggled the cuffs. "Thinks he can beat *me* up, after I walk in on him and Ms. College Perky Titties. Before I leave, I'd like to speak with your manager. I want to file a formal complaint that I could be held in here, getting my ass whooped and screaming, and not a single one from your staff came to see if there was a problem."

Smith cleared his throat. "Yes, ma'am. Right away. I'll get those removed and will find my manager posthaste."

"Damn straight, you will." She harrumphed and proffered her wrists. "I hope you have bolt cutters or something."

"Yeah, because room service always stows a pair of bolt cutters for these kinds of situations," he mumbled and walked farther into the room.

A cat meowed loudly as it ran past the opened door to this room, and Smith startled. He turned in time to see its long black tail disappear from view at the corner of the doorway, heading farther down the hallway. *Damn stray* ... He turned back to the woman, his heart pounding.

"Let me ask you something. Are you married?"

Smith scratched the back of his neck. "Yes."

"For a long time?"

"We have grandchildren."

"I bet you would never do this to her—cheat on her, then beat the snot out of her when she caught you."

"Ma'am, I think we all have our own demons, in our own ways. Let me see how thick those cuffs are." Smith approached the woman, noticing again how his tracks were the only impurities in the layers and layers of dust covering the floor.

She raised her wrists above her forehead so he wouldn't have to bend over to inspect their quality. "Hold on. Let me scoot up a bit." She wriggled her waist and hips so her back straightened against the wall furnace.

Smith grabbed the metal chain connecting the two cuffs and slightly tugged them closer to him. He felt the tautness of the connecting chain slacken, then he stumbled backward, still holding the chain but also the woman's two arms, severed at the shoulders. The momentum spilled him to his back on the floor, and both her arms—still cuffed at the wrists—fell on top of him.

"Look at what you fucking did to my arms, you dickhead!" The woman, now free from restraints, rose. "It wasn't enough that my good-for-nothing husband beat me up, but you have to take my arms!" She strode toward him and stopped directly over him. "I'm going to fucking eat you alive, old man."

Smith raised his hands in defense—the woman's arms flopping onto the floor next to him.

As she leaned forward, her mouth now open for human feasting, her chin hit her chest and didn't stop there. Her head rolled forward, disconnecting from her neck, and landed on Smith's chest.

He frantically swatted at the decapitated head and scooted backward to get away from it.

The woman's body crumpled to the floor, her gaze fixed on Smith. "I will eat your soul, you sonofabitch!"

Smith spider-walked backward from the room and into the hallway. As soon as he was clear of the doorway, the door slammed shut on its own. He let his backside fall to the floor, giving his hands and feet a rest from crawling backward and upside down. He gripped his shirt over his chest again and focused on his breathing.

"Help me!" the woman screamed from behind the closed door again. "Is someone out there? Please be out there!"

The buzzing from the neon Vertigo Motel sign increased. Smith stuck fingers in both his ears to muffle the sound. He glanced across the lobby at the flashing sign and noticed all his footprints and any previous actions that made marks in the dust were gone—erased. The dust was pristine again, like a snow-covered field before anyone or anything trampled across it.

"Yep, there's your answer, Smith, you old fool. You are certainly dead, and this is a very real Hell."

He clambered to his feet, his old bones creaking and screaming for reprieve.

"Help me!" a different person called out, not from the same room as Stepp's wife.

Smith glanced to the next door down the hallway.

"Help me! Is someone out there? Please be there!"

He tilted his head as he studied the door. The voice was familiar. But not one he had heard in what felt like forever.

"I can hear you out there! *Please* help me!"

Smith's eyes widened as he stepped backward. "No. No. How could it be?" He glanced behind him at the front door to the Vertigo, calculating the distance and how long it would take him to reach the outside—that was if the motel *would* let him leave.

"Why did you do it?" the woman asked. "We could've talked it out."

"Oh God," Smith muttered. "Wendy, I don't know what happened. I blacked out. I was suffering from a lot of blackouts during that time." He inched toward the door as he yelled loud enough so she heard him through the door. "It crushed me when I came home and saw you two together in our bed! The next thing I remember, I was in my truck with a shovel, covered in blood, and you were buried somewhere!"

The woman cackled. "You sure found it easy to move on afterward. Wynne seems like a nice piece of—"

Smith growled as he closed the distance as fast as he could and barreled through the motel room door.

On the bed lay Wendy, blood oozing from a hole in her forehead, a broken lamp on the floor. "Returning to the scene of the crime, honeybunches?" His dead naked wife cackled again, like the Wicked Witch of the West, and pointed. "Your expression is priceless."

Smith shook his head and shuffled backward through the door. "This isn't real. This is just a dream."

"Or your own private hell," Wendy added, sitting upright in the bed. "Here in the Vertigo, we all ride the carousel of truth. *Truth!*"

Smith entered the hallway and glanced at the next door farther down the hallway, wondering what truth lay behind that door. And the door after that. And the door after that.

"Mr. Arbuckle? Is that you out there?" A young girl's tiny voice came from the room behind him on the opposite side of the hallway.

Smith spun. "Oh God, no." To the Covingtons, he had been Todd Arbuckle.

"Mr. Arbuckle? Please help me if you're out there. My skin burns, and my baby elephant nightgown smells like it's burning."

Smith covered his mouth with his hand and gasped, tears welling in his eyes. "Rose ... oh sweet little Rose. I'm so, so sorry."

"*Please*, Mr. Arbuckle! It's starting to hurt, and I don't know how to get down! Where's Mommy? Just open the door so you can save me!"

"Rose! Rose, honey! I'll get some help! Just ... Just hang tight!" Smith spun toward the lobby and galloped toward the front entrance. He passed the reception desk, and a quick movement from his peripheral vision caught his eye.

The black-feathered wing of a vulture disappeared through the doorway to the back office, leaving a man standing behind the reception desk, his back turned toward Smith.

Smith stopped, his heartbeat pounding in his ears, and reached into his pocket. He removed the Polaroid and set it on the desk. "I don't know who you are or what this place really is, but I had nothing to do with Rose's sacrifice! If you are in charge here or are the one creating these apparitions, I promise you that you'll have no further problems from me."

The man behind the desk slowly turned to face Smith.

Smith's shoulders slumped, and he shook his head. "Oh, for Pete's sake. *You?* So this is what Anya meant when she said she had one final gift for me. You're to replace Tony."

Drool leaked from the corner of Stepp's half-opened mouth. His chest cavity was devoid of anything—blood, tissue, muscle—from where Anya had ripped out his heart as revenge for his final act of indignity. Stepp swayed slightly, like a flower in a summer breeze.

"So, you're my new bantling. Wonderful. I don't suppose you know how to get out of Dimension Vertigo and back to eighty-four, do you?"

Stepp swayed, unblinking.

"Didn't think so. Oh, your ex-wife is in room one. I think she'd *loooooove* to see you again."

Stepp's head slightly turned in that direction.

"Looks like you and I have more in common than I originally thought. C'mon, twinkle toes. Let's get out of—" Smith clenched his chest as he heard the beeping from a faraway machine and a sound that resembled someone using a cattle prod.

The *zap* sounded again, and his back involuntarily arched while his limbs stiffened, then went limp. Afterward, he heard the ambulance siren and felt warm, human—alive—hands compressing his chest.

"C'mon, Dad. Stay with us."

Travis ...

SALEM, MASSACHUSETTS; 1984

2: COMMITTED TO A BRIGHT FUTURE

Melissa shrugged her backpack onto her shoulder to keep it from falling any farther down her arm and stuck out her thumb at the oncoming traffic. She had reached US Route 95 South on foot but realized quickly she needed something that traveled faster than a teenage girl's legs, especially if she were to get anywhere out of the searchable vicinity. She crossed her fingers that any Goody Two-Shoes who might be concerned about a young girl hitchhiking and who might inform the local authorities would roll on by and that only a Good Samaritan willing to help her in her cause would stop to pick her up.

The next batch of headlights approached, and she leaned the top of her body across the fog line to be more visible to the drivers. She just needed one … The gaggles of vehicles sped past, kicking slush onto her pants, without stopping. The sound of engines and tires rolling faded, and Melissa hefted her bag again before trudging southbound.

Images of the metal-adorned, maroon-colored, leather-bound book of spells and the bronze horse paperweight inside her bag consumed her thoughts as she walked. Flashes of Vicki's bloodied head and Stepp's disconnected heart back at the attorney's office, plus her grandfather's body lying on her bedroom floor, superimposed themselves over the here and now of the dark highway.

She smirked when her thoughts landed on the realization that she was poised to be Anya's successor and may inherit her power and knowledge, once the witch successfully located the *real* Chosen One and becomes immortal—divine.

A blur of black caught her eye, and she looked skyward. She stopped walking to focus on the small tornado-like swirl of a kettle of vultures overhead.

As if the vultures realized Melissa had spotted them, they descended toward the highway shoulder. They gracefully landed a few yards ahead of her and approached in unison.

The intimidation and fear Melissa would once have felt in the vultures' presence was now replaced with a calmness and a sense of possessiveness. "Lookin' for me?"

The vultures stopped and bobbed their heads.

"Alright, fine. I'll come to you." Melissa headed toward where they had stopped and stood in front of them.

The lead vulture cocked its head and, with a chin lift, gestured to the backpack around her shoulder.

Melissa pointed to the strap. "You want something in here?"

The vulture darted its head to the other side, as if in confirmation.

Melissa let the bag slump to her bent elbow, unzipped it, and reached inside. "Did Anya send you for the book? Because she gave it to me. I'm keeping it safe until we can find the real sacrifice."

The lead vulture flapped its wings without taking flight.

"See?" Melissa removed the book and cradled it in the crook of her other elbow. "It's safe."

The vultures yapped in unison and launched into the sky as Melissa felt a hand on her shoulder. Black fabric fluttered in her peripheral vision.

"Do we have a destination, or are we just migrating south for the winter?"

Melissa chortled as she turned toward the pale face behind the black veil. "Just trying to get outta here as fast and as quietly as possible."

"And, by *quietly*, you mean, leaving a wake of arson, murder, and witchcraft as you depart?" Anya nodded. "Sounds like a solid plan, sport."

Melissa harrumphed and resumed walking again. "Can you *ever* discuss something without being sarcastic first? It's getting old."

"Funny," Anya said, keeping pace behind her apprentice. "Your grandfather said the same thing to me for decades. Guess you can't teach old cats new tricks."

"Don't talk about him right now."

"I saw what you did." Anya quickened her step and walked alongside Melissa now. "I was dealing with Baron— damn nosy, wannabe warlock barkeep—when you were … handling Smith. I reviewed it later."

Melissa eyed Anya. "Is he dead?"

"Do you care?"

Melissa stared at the ground and tightened her lips, considering the question.

"You must not, or you would've answered right—"

"I don't know! Okay? I don't know how I feel anymore."

Anya lovingly put her hand on Melissa's elbow. "Maybe you were too young to bring into the fold. I should have waited."

"I didn't expect all the … carnage to happen so fast. At Stepp's office, at my house. Everything was going to plan, then *poof!* Everything spun out of control." She swiped the length of her sleeve under her nose to catch the snot and tears mixed with the snow flurries that had collected on her upper lip. "We had the Chosen One. Dead to rights."

"Sometimes things change. And we have to change with them."

"Thanks, *Mom*." Melissa rolled her eyes.

They walked in silence until the sound of another batch of vehicles overshadowed the crunch of the snow under their soles.

"You gonna do that thumb thingy?" Anya asked, watching the procession of cars pass.

"*Nah*, I want to walk right now. Clear my thoughts."

Anya nodded. "You do know who you're walking with, right?"

"What's that supposed to mean?"

Anya shook her head. "I won't ask you again, child. Where are you headed? I know you have picked somewhere, so don't give me the 'anywhere but here' line. I can see right through you."

Melissa sighed. "Thought I'd go see Uncle Hank in Vegas."

"Whatever for? That old coot is closer to death than Smith."

Melissa halted. "So ... Grandpapa is still alive?"

Anya studied Melissa from the corner of her eye. "You do care!"

"Yeah ..." She kicked a pebble into the roadway. "A little."

"He's alive but not yet stable. And again, why Hank?"

"Uncle Hank has always been there for me. And he lives far enough away where I could hide out there. And I think he'd protect me. He wouldn't rat me out to my parents."

"And how are you so sure?"

"I dunno." Melissa shrugged and continued walking. "Just a hunch. Uncle Hank's ... different."

"And you thought a teenage girl, during the holidays, would just easy-peasy hitchhike almost three thousand miles without as much as an eyebrow raise? Do you know how many drivers you'd need?"

"I was hoping to get lucky."

Anya choked on her laugh as the fabric from her black robe flapped behind her in the wind. "Lucky enough to find that one schmuck who's driving from Massachusetts to Nevada? You are thick, child. What if an unsavory character tried anything inappropriate?"

"I have Dad's gun. I found it in his sock drawer."

"You just have all the answers. Got it *all* figured out, huh?"

"And I'm powerful now."

Anya scoffed. "Don't get cocky."

"Like you did with Rose Covington?" Melissa eyed the witch. "Plus, I can shoot laser beams from my eyes to move things."

"Ah, yes. Poor Madam Hapney's beloved desk."

Both women giggled together.

"Now that I am Stepp's replacement and the Mushroom Cult leader, I also thought it would be fitting to return the operation to Vegas, where my family's involvement started."

"So, this is a sentimental full-circle kind of thing? I didn't peg you for the sort. But I like your moxie, child. Sit back and enjoy the ride."

"What—"

Before Melissa could finish her question, everything turned purple, and she felt like her bones had accelerated faster than her skin was traveling.

3: 9 TO 5 AT THE MORGUE

Christopher Harth tucked the rolled-up newspaper under his armpit so he could flip the light switch to the morgue. Incandescent bulbs turned on in a scattered pattern, illuminating the metal tables and the cadavers that had been delivered during the night. He surveyed the two new bodies and sighed. Harth cleared his throat—the sound echoing off the far wall of body-size drawers—and headed for the Mr. Coffee. He set his newspaper next to the carafe and contemplated just finishing the pot from yesterday or brewing a new one.

A knock on the opened door startled him from his decision, and he turned toward the entrance.

"G'morning, Chris." Sergeant Santana entered the room and proffered a fresh steaming cup of coffee. "Thought you might need this."

"Thanks, Sarge." He reached for the cup and turned toward the first of the covered bodies. "One of these must be a person of interest, if you're here at the crack of dawn."

"I wanted to be here when you looked at that one." He pointed with his chin to a table. "We don't know what happened, and it's pretty gruesome. Plus, it's …" Santana looked at the floor.

"Someone we know?"

"It's Baron. From the Pale Horse."

"Oh, jeez." Harth's shoulders slumped.

"We found him in his back office, mauled."

"Mauled?"

Santana approached the table and slid back the top of the sheet, exposing Baron's face. "No animal around here could have done this."

Harth cocked his head and squinted. "Looks like a school of piranhas ate him alive. What about the rest of his body?" Harth pulled the sheet farther down but stopped when Santana answered.

"Not a scratch. It's like whoever did this only wanted to remove his face."

Harth lifted Baron's head and felt underneath while staring at the far wall. "No damage or lacerations to the back of his head."

"No. The entire assault was to his face. The rest of his body was left untouched."

Harth eyed the sergeant. "The Wharf Killer again?"

"Doesn't fit his MO."

"Looks like I'll be making that fresh pot of coffee after all. I'll be here a while." Harth sipped from the cup that Santana had given him, then set the cup on the nearby counter. "Poor guy. Really liked him too. Never seemed to cause any problems."

"He's been a solid staple in the community for as long as I can remember. One of the good ones. I'm sure he even helped us, with the way he ran the Pale Horse, not letting arguments escalate to violence."

Harth's gaze shot to Santana. "Was anyone after him? Any word on the street of anything shady?"

"The guy was clean as a whistle. Respected by all, loved by more."

Harth nodded and took another sip. "Thanks for the joe, Sarge."

"I'll check back with you later. If anything pops before I call you, could you let me know as soon as possible? Those teeth marks seem so … insidious."

"Teeth marks?" Harth abandoned his coffee and turned to Baron's mutilated face and bent closer. "What in the …?" He touched one of the thousands of indentations in Baron's flesh.

"I'll leave ya to it, Chris." Santana turned and strode toward the door.

"I'll call if I find anything," Harth mumbled—too quietly for the sergeant to hear as the door closed—leaving the medical examiner alone with the cadavers.

Harth plopped into the black-cushioned seat on wheels and rolled himself backward to the radio on the counter. He extended the antennae and flipped the switch to hear the Bee Gees already into the second verse of "How Deep is Your Love?" He collected a few surgical instruments and glided himself back to Baron's body.

"Let's see if we can figure out what happened to you, bud. What a shame." Harth leaned closer to Baron's face and touched the edges of one of the divots in the flesh with a metal pick. He got the tip of the pick under the open wound and lifted the skin so he could inspect the laceration marks. "What kind of animal …?"

The Bee Gees ended, and the DJ's voice came from the single-speaker radio. "Let's put away those bellbottoms for a bit and get into the holiday spirit. With Christmas just around the corner, here is one for all you ladies and gents who might be standing under the mistletoe without anyone to kiss this year. Just know you aren't alone. You'll always have the king! Take it away, Elvis."

Harth glanced at the radio, as if the DJ could hear him. "Oh, no. Not this early in the morning." He rolled the chair toward the counter as the opening melody of "Blue Christmas" filled the morgue. Harth leaned forward to dial through the stations.

Static. Country. *Static.* New wave. *Static.* Oldies. *Static.* Sports. *Static.* Rock. *Stop.*

Harth rose from the chair and ran his fingers through his hair as he hummed along to "That's All" by Genesis. Harth released a long sigh and took a few gulps of the black coffee. He put one hand on his hip and glanced at the wall clock—9:00 a.m. He turned to survey Baron's body again, and the coffee cup dropped from his hand, landing with a *splat* on the tiled floor.

Harth attempted to take another step backward, even though he was already pressed against the counter. "What in the holy hell?" He inched slowly, the counter still pressing into his waist, toward the farthest wall from the tables. His feet pivoted back and forth, without losing contact with the floor, to move him sideways.

He reached the wall phone, snatched the receiver, and dialed Santana's number by heart. Every ring in the earpiece sounded like it lasted an hour before the brief spot of silence and the next ring. Finally, he heard the other end *click* open.

"Salem PD, Sergeant Santana speaking."

"Sarge …"

"Chris? Is that you?"

"Sarge …" Harth swallowed hard. "You need to come here right now. Baron's body is gone."

"Baron's body is … *what*? It sounded like you said— Okay, Judy! Give me a minute. I'll bring Chief McBrayer the file as soon as I'm off the phone … Yeah, that's fine … No, let him go home … Sorry, Chris. Can you repeat that?"

Harth's fingers tightened around the receiver until his knuckles whitened. "He's *gone*! I turned my back for a second, and the table is empty!"

"Jesus Christ. Calm down. I'll be right there. I think you've been working too hard. There's something to be said for a nine-to-five schedule, not a nine-to-midnight, like you've been pulling."

"For fuck's sake, Sarge! The body is not here!"

"Sit tight … Hey, Raynard! Can you fire up a cruiser and take me to the morgue?"

Harth heard another voice answer from the background at the other end of the call.

"Alright, me and Raynard are on our way."

Harth removed the phone from his ear and hung it on its base without averting his gaze from the vacant metal table. He slowly approached the discarded sheet on the floor. He leaned forward to glance through the door's small window for any intruders—or walking dead—before picking up the sheet.

Turning it over in his hands, he noticed the bloodstains on it from Baron's face. He balled up the sheet and tossed it onto the metal table.

Harth spun toward the other cadaver. "Do you plan on leaving too?" He shook his head and chuckled at the absurd way his morning was unfolding.

The radio blended the ending of Genesis into the intro of the Misfits' "Night of the Living Dead."

Almost instinctively, Harth grabbed the tray of instruments and hurled it like a frisbee at the radio, his heart hammering in his ears and his hands shaking. The tray collided with the radio, sending both to the tile floor and unplugging the radio from the socket, silencing the Misfits' song better suited for Halloween than Christmas. The only sound left in the room was the clanging of the tray still settling on the floor and Harth's rapid breathing.

The tray came to rest, and silence fell over the room. Harth grabbed the edge of the table and strained his ears to try to hear any movement in the hallway—even though he was certain the door had never opened. That meant … either the thief or the reanimated corpse were still in the room with him.

His gaze darted back and forth, quickly inventorying if anything was out of place or seemed amiss. Everything was in its rightful place. The sharp ticking of the second hand on the wall clock grew louder as the ambiance in the room seemed to close in on him. He rubbed the back of his neck, his fingers wiping away the thin layer of cold sweat he hadn't noticed before. He now regretted silencing the radio; any noise other than the subtle sounds of the morgue would be better right now—even if it were Glenn Danzig's baritone crooning during Christmastime.

Harth slowly crouched to peek under the metal table. Maybe the corpse had just fallen and was underneath? Would that be even creepier? He didn't know, but he saw nothing underneath the table. When he heard two car doors slam closed nearby outside, he straightened his back.

He exhaled what seemed to be more air than his lungs could hold as the door opened, and the two officers entered. He pointed to the empty table.

"What in God's green creation ...?" Officer Raynard asked as he stepped aside to let his sergeant get farther into the room.

Santana froze and stared wide-eyed at Harth. "Where the fuck is it?"

"I dunno."

"Alright, walk me through every step you took."

"I wheeled to the radio to change the radio station, took a sip of coffee, and when I turned around, he was gone."

Santana eyed Raynard. "Start taking photos, and don't move anything."

"I picked up the sheet from the floor, if you want to log that I had moved that after the body was gone."

Raynard nodded and jotted it on his notepad.

"And the tray?" Santana jutted his chin toward the mess on the floor.

Harth shrugged. "Didn't like the song."

Santana snickered and shook his head. "I guess we all need a little comic relief right now."

"I'll go call this in to the chief," Raynard said.

"Right. Then call for the detective unit." Santana faced Harth. "We should leave the room while he takes pictures and wait for the detectives. I want to wash my hands of this soup-sandwich and pass this onto someone's plate as fast as I can. This is giving me the heebie-jeebies."

"I'm right behind you."

"I'll need you to make an official statement, Chris. I hope you know that."

"Oh, I figured. Makes me wish we had a CCTV camera in here." Harth glanced at all four corners of the ceiling as he leaned forward to grab his coffee cup.

Santana patted Harth's back as they exited the room.

Trying to explain the situation to Chief McBrayer, Raynard's words faded as the door slowly swung closed behind Sarge and Chris, leaving them alone in the hallway.

4: EXPERIMENTS IN EMBRYOS

Smith's new bantling sat in the chair opposite Smith's hospital bed, a line of drool reaching from Stepp's lips to the floor.

Smith laid motionless, staring at the ceiling and listening to the machine that beeped in time with his heartbeat. Wires and tubes extended from his nose and arms. "Are you … a punishment for me, or am I a … punishment for you?" Smith asked, his voice hoarse and cracking. "Or does she … hate us equally now?"

Smith didn't expect a response—at least not one that involved words. He already missed Tony's chirps and grunts as replies. He wondered what kind of bantling Stepp would prove to be, or, better yet, how Smith could dismiss Stepp so Smith could live the rest of his life without taking care of anything in Anya's world.

Except, he knew that wasn't a possibility, not with his granddaughter Melissa under Anya's spell now.

Remembering how the previous night's events had played out caused him to hack and cough, and his chest tightened. The machines went wild.

The door burst open, and two nurses and his son strode into the room, right past Stepp.

"Dad?"

"Is he okay?" Smith heard his daughter-in-law, Gwen, ask.

"Just a coughing fit," one nurse said. "He's already calming down."

"Can he hear us?" Travis asked. "Dad?"

Smith made eye contact with his son.

"Oh, thank God." Travis squeezed Smith's hand. "You're going to be all right, Dad. Do you understand? Do you want me to get Mom? She's asleep in the waiting room."

Smith squeezed his son's hand. "Let … Let her … sleep."

"Don't talk, Mr. Smith," the nurse said as the other nurse surveyed the monitors. "Save your strength."

Smith sneaked a peek at Stepp sitting on the chair behind his family, staring absentmindedly at a spot on the wall—which the rising sun illuminated—before resuming his focus on the ceiling.

"I think someone might be at the office by now. I need to call out sick from work," Gwen said to Travis, checking the time on the wall clock.

Travis nodded as he watched his father's chest rise and fall with each shallow breath. When Gwen left the room to make the call, Travis shuffled backward and sat in the chair where Smith had last seen Stepp. Smith strained his eyes so he could see the chair and noticed Travis sitting with Stepp, then adjusting himself, while superimposed on top of each other.

Travis put his face in his hands. "You gave us a big scare, Dad. Melissa's giving us a bigger one. I spent all night looking for her. You were the last one to see her. If you remember anything—"

"Jumped …"

"What?" Travis stood; Stepp continued to drool onto the floor.

Smith turned his head toward his son. "She … jumped. From the"—a bout of hacking coughs sent the machines into a frenzy again—"window."

"The police saw the tracks in the snow." Travis sat again, Stepp not reacting to his lap buddy. "They followed them as far as they could through the woods but lost them. Do you have any idea where she might be headed? Did she say anything before she … jumped? If it's because of being blamed for that vandalism to the psychic's shop, we still don't know—"

The door opened, and Gwen entered the room, followed by Officer Taylor. "Work said to take as much time off as I needed. And Officer Taylor has some more questions for us."

Travis nodded and stood again, getting off Stepp's lap.

"This'll only take a minute, sir." Taylor flipped to the next blank page in his notepad. "Are there any weapons in the house? And if there are, can you confirm they are still there?"

Travis swallowed hard. "We don't have any guns, if that's what you're asking."

Taylor nodded, satisfied with the answer. "If you do find anything missing, anything with a serial number, please let us know so we can log it. That helps if someone tries to pawn it. Then we can track their location. It's not automatic, but it gives us a good travel pattern."

"We will. Thank you," Gwen said.

Officer Taylor excused himself and left the room.

"I gotta head home and check on something," Travis said.

Gwen reached for her jacket. "I'll come with you."

"That's a good idea." Smith coughed again. "You should stay there too … in case Mel comes home."

After Smith's family exited the room, followed by the nurses, he studied the chair where Stepp sat. "Do … Do you know where Anya is?" Smith stifled another round of coughs. "Because I think wherever … she is, Mel is nearby."

Stepp's gaze came off the wall and focused on Smith's face, and Stepp, for the first time, appeared to have better control over his muscles and his movements. He opened his mouth to speak, but all that came out was a chirp.

Smith chuckled to himself. *I knew it was only a matter of time.*

When Stepp bowed his head, he noticed the gaping hole in chest, and his eyebrows furrowed. He jumped to his feet, whining like a dog to come in from the rain, and spun, spun, spun around, trying to see where the other side of the hole went. He eyed Smith frantically, as if the answer lay with him, then stuck his right arm through the hole and grabbed the fingers of his left hand from the other side.

"You look … like a pretzel," Smith wheezed. "I hope you enjoy this room, because I think we're stuck here for a while."

Stepp neighed like a horse, unlinking his hands.

"At least … At least no one can … see you."

Stepp raised a finger to his lips, signaling for Smith to save his breath.

"I know what you did."

Stepp tilted his head.

"To your wife." A fit of coughs racked his body. "I saw it in the Vertigo. We aren't so different after all, you piece of crud."

Stepp whinnied and wagged an accusing finger at Smith.

"I'm going to kill you … a second time, when I get out of here and be done … with it all. Mark my words."

Stepp pouted and exaggeratedly bounced back and forth from foot to foot, flopping like a taunting marionette.

A doctor entered and headed straight for Smith's bedside. "I see you're awake. Are you feeling any discomfort?"

Smith shook his head without raising it from the pillow.

The doctor flipped the first page on the clipboard in his hands. "Good news is, you won't need surgery. Bad news is, we have no idea what caused the episode. Your heart is perfectly healthy, no blockage in any of the valves. Your blood pressure is within range. Your blood oxygen levels are healthy, and your cholesterol is better than someone half your age. On paper, you are fit as a fiddle. We can run some more labs to see if any underlying conditions exist, but, other than that, as soon as you regain your strength, I see no reason for you to stay here."

The door cracked open, and Wynn shambled into the room.

"Ah, Mrs. Smith. I was just reviewing the test results with your husband."

"Should I sit down?"

"All good things. He's as healthy as a horse."

Wynn interlaced her fingers with Smith's hand. "I've seen some pretty sick horses in my lifetime."

Smith chuckled and was forced to stop to catch his breath.

"His difficulty breathing should work itself out as he gets stronger. Will someone be at home who can take care of him?"

"Last time I checked, I hadn't bought the farm yet."

"No offense intended, Mrs. Smith. I just meant, if he fell or needed help moving."

"I think we'll do just fine." She squeezed Smith's hand.

"Perfect. We'll keep him here for a few days, just for observation, as a precaution, but everything looks good to go." The doctor tucked his clipboard under the crook of his arm and nodded before leaving the room.

Wynn rubbed her palm across Smith's forehead. "How you feeling?"

"Better."

"You gave us quite the scare."

He tugged on her arm, bringing her closer to his face. "We need to find Mel. She's gotten herself in deeper than she had expected."

"What? What are you talking about? What do you *know*? Do you know where she is?"

Smith shook his head. "No, but I know why she left."

Wynn raised an eyebrow and cocked her head. "Spill it, mister."

Smith debated where he should start. From the very beginning? And where exactly was that beginning? Was it moving to Salem all those years ago? Was it being the Wharf Killer? Was it co-conspiring with George Covington's killings at the Desert Palms Motel? Was it getting tangled in Anya's web of deceit? Was it helping feed the Mushroom Cult with new recruits? Or did he reveal his whole hand and start with Wendy's death, before he had even met Wynn? How much did he owe his wife, and how much did she *need* to know? Was there a line where she would still understand, but, if crossed, he would become a monster to her?

"Well?" Wynn tapped her foot.

Smith took a deep breath and closed his eyes. "Mel had befriended a self-proclaimed witch downtown. They were having secret meetings, and this witch was supposedly teaching her spells and fantasy powers." He opened his eyes. "All hogwash, charlatan stuff. But Mel got sucked into it. I know she set fire to that psychic's desk. She told me. That's why she ran."

"So, that's all this is over? Some two-bit wannabe witch who Mel got involved with?"

Smith nodded, the fabric of the pillow scratching the back of head, as well as his conscience.

"Where does this so-called witch live? Has anyone checked there? Maybe she's shacking up with her until this blows over."

"I don't know where she lives, doll. I don't"—the coughs shook the whole bed, and the frame banged against the wall—"even know the witch's name."

"Well ..." Wynn bit her fingernail. "At least it's something to go on. It's more than we had a few minutes ago."

"From Mel's description, I don't trust this new friend. I don't think she'd harm Mel, per se, but I have a gut feeling she will be an incredibly bad influence. Will coerce Mel into doing things she normally wouldn't."

"Like ... illegal stuff?"

"Who knows, but I hope the police, when they find her, realize this witch had a lot of influence over Mel and don't hold Mel accountable for any mistakes or decisions she might be making right now." Smith closed his eyes and recalled how Mel had sewn his lips shut just before his heart gave out. The power she had exhibited had been surprising.

"Would the psychic know who this witch is?"

Smith contemplated, again, how much he should reveal. But it seemed one white lie could snowball into an avalanche if he continued to give any answers other than *I don't know*, so he shrugged.

"I love you. Don't give me a scare like that again."

Smith squeezed her hand and nodded.

"I'll leave you so you can get some rest. I'll have the nurses' station call the police station so I can relay to them what you told me. Even though it's not much, any bit of info can help, right, Detective?"

Smith chuckled, and it ignited another round of hacking.

She kissed his forehead and headed for the hallway.

When the door closed behind her, Smith scanned the room for his bantling. He found Stepp sitting on the chair, holding a magazine high to obscure his face, looking like someone reading while waiting for their name to be called.

"Oh, so, you can read now?"

Stepp leaned his head to the side without moving the magazine from his face so he could see the bed. He turned the opened magazine around to show Smith what page he had been reading. A full-size ad for *Breakin' 2: Electric Boogaloo* stared back at Smith, and Stepp pointed to the large boombox in the picture.

"Some nights I'd like to forget. That is one of them. Do you remember being there? With that girl who dumped her bucket of popcorn on you? Yeah, you were just being you and doing what you do best." Smith stopped talking to catch his breath.

Stepp eyed the ad again and wiped some drool off his chin. He slammed the magazine on the floor as hard as he could and stood.

"You are nothing like Tony," Smith said and closed his eyes. "Now, if you don't mind, I'd like to get some sleep. Go away to wherever you guys go for a bit and leave me be. In fact"—Smith opened one eye to watch Stepp—"go wherever it is you abominations go and don't ever come back." He waved the back of his hand at the bantling. "Shoo!"

Stepp clenched both hands into fists and grunted.

Smith opened the other eye. "Do you not know how to get there on your own, or do you need Anya to show you first? Because, I'll be honest with ya, I'll go mad if you can't leave and need to stick around until you're shown. I don't think Anya is coming back."

Stepp cocked his head at the sound of the witch's name.

"*No sirree bop.* I think she left you for me as a parting gift." He closed both eyes. "I am done with her, and when I get out of this hospital, if you're still lingering around, I'll kill you and be done with you too."

Stepp whined and stuck out his tongue at the old detective in the bed.

Smith raised the upper part of his torso to address Stepp one last time before going back to sleep, but the ghoul was gone.

5: WATCHING YOU

"You know that we can use the netherworld to travel anywhere we want to go," Anya said to Melissa right after they materialized in the Mushroom Cult's realm. "How do you think we appear and disappear so quickly?"

"So, are we in Vegas right now?" Melissa asked, beholding the purple hues of the witch's netherworld.

"Almost. There's still a process we must—" Anya placed a hand on Melissa's chest to halt the girl.

"What is—"

Anya shushed her and squinted as she scanned the realm. "Something's not right. Someone's … here."

"Who?" Melissa whispered.

Anya strode forward and entered another spatial dimension within the realm.

Melissa followed and noticed a large throne in the middle of the area, then saw multiple staggered limbs, all waving and protruding from what looked like a massive spiderweb against the far wall.

"Don't just stand there. Help me!" Anya yelled as she jogged toward the wall of web, her black robe floating behind her, as if on waves.

Melissa obeyed and headed for the wall. As she approached, she recognized the Mushroom Cultists pinned against the wall underneath the web.

Anya floated up to meet the top row of waving limbs. "You free Pum'kin, and I'll get Cyana down."

Melissa grabbed the lower part of the web and tested it for strength. When she was confident it would hold her weight, she reached her hands upward and placed her feet on the bottom of the web. She strategically climbed the webbing, as if she were rock climbing back in summer camp.

Cyana whizzed past Melissa's head.

She looked up at Anya and saw the witch hanging on the web, one hand on the edge of a large divot where Cyana had been trapped like a fly.

"Hurry and cut Pum'kin loose. They can't stay like this for long. It's cutting off their circulation."

Melissa reached her flailing target. "How do I cut her loose? I don't have anything with me!"

"You wanna be a witch, right? Use those laser beams you were bragging about," Anya retorted and climbed down the webbing to the next ghoul trapped like a spider.

Melissa took a deep breath and focused all her energy into the webbing holding Pum'kin's torso. She pursed her lips and squinted, trying to concentrate.

"I got Nikki free. How's it coming down there?"

"Don't interrupt me. I'm working on it." Melissa glared harder at the webbing.

A moment later, Cinnamon fell to the ground, narrowly missing Melissa on the plummet downward.

"That's three. How's it coming with Pum'kin?"

"Just … fucking hold on!"

"You are failing me, child. Your boasting about your powers seems to be all for naught. Don't make me lose faith in you."

Melissa tightened her core and shot the witch a death stare. "I'm working on it," she replied through gritted teeth.

"Work harder. We can't afford to lose my top lieutenant."

Melissa relaxed her muscles. "If she's so important to you, then why the fuck did you leave her for me to free?"

"The test is more important than the ghoul. If we lose her, then you have also lost. And I'll have no use for either of you."

"Bitch," Melissa muttered.

"Okay, number four, my final girl, heading your way." Anya sliced her long fingernail across the webbing, and Candy crashed to the ground. "How's it going?"

Melissa exhaled loudly. "I can't. You gotta help her. I thought I could, but I—"

Anya swiped Melissa off the webbing, sending the teenager to the ground, and had Pum'kin freed within mere seconds. Anya floated gracefully to the floor, her cult lieutenant slung over her shoulder. "Get up, child."

Melissa studied the witch from the ground before she climbed to her feet. She slapped away the dust from her jeans and met Anya's gaze.

Anya gently lowered Pum'kin to the ground and watched as the five ghouls collected themselves, reoriented their surroundings, and chirped at the witch and the teenager in gratitude.

"Oh no," Anya said. "Don't you thank *her*." She eyed Melissa. "She was almost the cause of your demise."

The five ghouls cocked their heads in unison, like puppies, and regarded Melissa.

Melissa shook her head and looked at the floor. "Thanks for telling them that."

"You need to win their trust, child." Anya wrapped an arm around Melissa's shoulders. "Because once it's won, it's forever. And they will go to the ends of the Earth for you— they will even die for you. But you can't earn it if they think you might ever, and I mean *ever*, fail them."

"Is that the kind of bullshit you're feeding this young girl's head with?" a man with a deep voice asked from the other side of Anya's throne.

Melissa quickly eyed Anya for answers to what was happening and who that was.

Anya slowly circled to her throne to identify the imposter. As she shuffled around, his black leather pants and black boots came into view. She quickened her pace to stand in front of her uninvited guest, who deigned to sit on her throne. "*You!* I fucking ate your face."

Baron crossed his legs and exaggeratedly wiggled in Anya's throne, ensuring she saw how comfortable and unintimidated he was.

"How did you even get in here?"

Baron spied Melissa from the corner of his eye. "I've been watching you, girl. You have made some poor choices recently about the company you keep." His focus landed on Anya. "Are you still so naive to think someone as meek as you could ever kill me? I've been around a lot longer than you, and I will continue to be around, long after you're gone."

Anya took an aggressive step closer. "You robbed me of the Chosen One, and I will never forgive you."

"That was centuries ago, you old hag." Baron surveyed the space. "I like what you've done to the place. Been a while since I was in here."

Anya growled and opened her mouth to reveal her three rows of fangs.

Melissa's eyes widened, and she stepped backward.

"Oh, knock off the theatrics." Baron rose from the throne and clasped his hands behind his back as he paced the area, his back to the fanged witch, while he eyed Melissa. "I don't think we've been properly introduced. My name is Baron, High Priest of the Mushroom Cult. And I can use the moon as my eyes." He waved his hand at the throne room's abstract ceiling, and a full moon appeared, as if hanging from a string. He waved his hand again, and the moon vanished.

"High Priest of the Mushroom ... I don't understand." Melissa looked at Anya for answers to the witch's recent vampiric transformation and Baron's proclamation.

"You are no high priest of *anything*," Anya spat. "And you certainly don't have any control over my girls."

Baron tsked and removed a black-veiled voodoo doll from his pocket. He leaned close to Melissa and said softly, "She still underestimates me, even after all these years." He spun and pointed at the witch. "I've always believed in a balance of light and dark, good and evil. An overabundance of good in the world can lead to a knee-jerk reaction of atrocities."

Anya hissed but remained in her spot as she watched Baron cradle the voodoo doll in her likeness in one hand and raise a pin in the other. "Don't you even think about it, or I will eat the rest of your body, like I should have last night."

"Such an infant …" Baron lowered the pin toward the Anya doll's stomach. The pin flung from his fingers, clanked against the side wall, and fell to the ground. Baron looked quickly at the teenage human.

"I don't know who you are, but you are a liar, and you need to leave us alone." Melissa stepped toward the warlock. She squinted at his hand, and the doll launched across the room and landed on Anya's throne.

"That's my girl," Anya muttered and tugged her veil just a little more to cover her face.

Baron chuckled and shook his head. "Your window for saving your soul is closing, girl. If you don't break free from Anya's spell soon, nefariousness will befall you. And I might not help you anymore."

"Don't let him leave, child, until I have eaten his soul." Anya quickened her pace toward the intruder.

"Girls, get him!" Melissa ordered the cult.

With her command activating their full potential, the five ghouls stormed Baron.

Baron's gaze bounced from Anya to the ghouls to Melissa, all approaching from different angles. He reached inside his trench coat and retrieved a maroon-colored, leather-bound book. He waved it above his head, and the ghouls halted—so did Melissa.

"What is that? How does he have the book?" Melissa eyed Anya.

"That's not our book, child. It's one full of half-truths and plagiarism. We hold the only true book."

"This book, Melissa," Baron explained, "has been written by the purest of hearts. It is magic divine. This is the only divine book. Your mentor's book is comprised of only wishes and diluted spells."

"Oh, yeah? Then how did I set Madam Hapney's desk on fire? How did I seal shut Grandpapa's lips and stop his heart?" Melissa put her hands on her hips. "And how did I rip your doll from your hands, if the spells are so diluted?"

"Like you freed that one"—Baron pointed at Pum'kin—"from my web?"

Anya shrieked a war cry and lunged at the warlock.

Baron raised his book in defense and opened it so the pages pointed at the incoming witch.

Orange light exploded from the pages, like a spotlight, flinging Anya across the throne room and against the wall still covered in webbing.

Baron closed the book with a slam and approached the wall.

"Let her go!" Melissa screamed but became preoccupied, her feet glued and unable to rise off the ground.

"I'll be with you next," he said as he passed the stuck teenager toward his way to the wall.

Anya had landed upside down and diagonal against the webbing, arms splayed, as if she were on a spinning wheel, partaking of a circus knife-throwing act. She panted and strained as she tried to pull any limb free from the webbing.

Baron cocked his head and bent far enough down so he was face to face with the witch. "You may win the little battles sometimes, Anya, but you'll never win the war." He rubbed his reconstructed facial skin. "I am too powerful to be bested by you."

Anya got control of her breathing and retracted her three rows of fangs. "All I've ever aspired to be was immortal. Divine, like you. Are you so threatened by sharing that divinity with someone that you feel the need to keep getting in my way? I'm not even bothering you or stepping on your toes. Why can't you share what you have? It's no skin off your back!"

"I've turned a blind eye to most of your shenanigans. To your so-called cult." Baron rose to an upright position and spied the ghouls. "To your control over the vultures. But when it comes to your attempt to become like *me*, we will always have problems. This town ain't big enough for the two of us." Baron tucked his book into his trench coat and waved his hand at Melissa.

She felt her feet become unstuck and almost toppled over.

"You can come with me right now, girl, and I can show you the true power of the book. Or you can stay here and run the risk of falling so far from redemption that I fear you might become collateral damage. It's your choice. I won't force you, because then I'd always know your decision was not made with your heart."

Melissa's gaze panned between the large ominous man standing in front of her and the trapped helpless-looking witch stuck to the webbing in her own throne room. Who was more powerful? Who would have better success at paving Mel's path toward regency? One of the beings before her had consistently failed their mission, and the other seemed indestructible and infallible.

Just as she had chosen one in her mind, a cloud of black feathers stormed into the throne room seemingly from nowhere. The vultures engulfed Baron with snapping beaks and hissing until they obscured every inch of his body.

Anya cackled from the wall. "I'm more than just an old hag, Baron. I have tricks up every sleeve."

The whirlpool of vultures collapsed into itself, revealing an empty space where Baron had once stood, and the birds of prey landed in scattered groups within the room.

Anya fell from the wall and landed on her head with an *oomph*. She rose and readjusted her black veil over her pale face. She clap-slapped her hands, as if they had dust to be rid of. "I guess he didn't see that coming. Baron might be immortal, but he's not unbeatable within the moment. Thanks for sticking with me, child. Your loyalty was not unrecognized."

Melissa nodded once and stared at the ground, her heart hammering in her ears and uncertainty swimming in her head. She spied the Anya doll still sitting on the witch's throne—a crude mini-version of her mentor—slumped sideways and pathetic.

LAS VEGAS, NEVADA; 1984

6: (STILL) LOOKIN' FOR LOVE

Hank unlocked the front door to Steel's Taco Shed and ambled into his restaurant. He flipped on the lights, tossed his keys onto the serving counter, and leaned his walking cane against a table. He flipped through the envelopes of mail that his shift manager had left for him from yesterday. Not seeing anything of significance, he tossed the pile onto the counter, and they slid, fanning out.

He rubbed his wrinkled and liver-spotted hands together for warmth against the chilly Las Vegas morning. He checked the wall clock, shaped like a crunchy taco, and calculated how much time he had before the early lunch shift employees would start to arrive. He nodded and sauntered into his office. He plopped his weary bones into his desk chair and bent forward to dial the combination of the safe. It cracked open, and he retrieved the nightly deposit from inside. He matched the bills against the ledger, satisfied it was all there.

This location was run like a well-oiled machine, not like his newly opened location in Lynn, where the tragedy of his night manager Roxanne had already stained his reputation in Massachusetts in less than one year of the grand opening. He didn't want to, but he saw no choice but to close the Lynn location and to live out whatever years—or months—he had left, reaping the benefits and profits from this location.

The rapping at the front door distracted him from his thoughts, and he rose on shaky legs to see who was there. When he recognized the silhouette on the other side of the glass front door, he smiled and waved. He shuffled to the front of the Taco Shed and unlocked the door decorated in decals of Mexican hats and shredded lettuce.

"Brought you a coffee," Floyd said, entering the dining room.

"With or without a shot?" Hank asked, flashing a smirk at his next-door business owner and current heartthrob, before his emphysema racked him into a coughing fit.

"Silly goose!" Floyd playfully nudged Hank's arm.

Hank swallowed hard to settle his lungs and stared at the spot where Floyd had touched him for a little longer than normal. "Where are you headed this morning?"

"Got a chess game in the park in thirty minutes. That whippersnapper has my number every time. One day, I'll beat him."

Hank laughed harder than was warranted. "Us old fogies can't keep up with them kids anymore. Too many generations removed."

"And they're so much smarter than we were at their age, with their VCHs and cassette boxes."

"You mean, VHSs and boomboxes."

Floyd chortled. "See if you don't have a pulse on what's groovy right now."

"Yeah. And *groovy* is not groovy to say anymore, love! That's so twenty years ago." Hank blushed, hoping he didn't sound too flirtatious, especially with a term of endearment that came so naturally to him. He paused to gauge Floyd's reaction. It looked like it had gone unnoticed. "Now it's *hip* or *gnarly*."

"And this is why I keep you around." Floyd chuckled and raised his coffee cup, as if to say, *Cheers!*

"Yep." Hank looked at the floor and kicked a lone piece of onion from last night's supper rush. "That's why you keep me around …"

"You okay, pal? You seem a little blue. Is that okay to still say? *Blue*? I mean, colors will never go out of vogue with the young'ins, right?"

Hank laughed and wished he could truly confess. "I've just had a rough time at my Boston-area location this week. Feels like the weight on my shoulders is getting too heavy to carry myself," Hank half-lied, hoping Floyd would buy that as the sole reason for his mood and also hoping Floyd would offer comfort—in any form.

"It's tough being a business owner nowadays, especially at our age. If I didn't have my grandchildren around to help run Castaway's, the eatery would've gone under a long time ago. Or I would have died from a heart attack."

Hank flexed his lips against his teeth—not the answer he was looking for. "Yeah, I guess you're right." He tried to will himself to snap out of his funk; wearing his emotions on his sleeve in front of Floyd was no way to land this catch. "Oh, you. Always teasing us about our ages. As if Father Time had any say over this bod!" He knew that sounded forced because it *felt* forced.

A car door slammed nearby, and Floyd turned toward the parking lot, then took a long sip of his coffee. "Well, looks like your crew is coming in, ready to make *dem* tacos."

"You tease, but you know my tacos are the best tacos you'll ever taste, love." *Golly, did he catch the double meaning in that? I'm so stupid.*

Floyd eyed him warily. "Hard or soft?"

"Huh?" Hank's gaze snapped to Floyd's artificially suntanned face and white hair.

Floyd leaned in and whispered, "Do you think I'd like your hard tacos or your soft tacos better?"

Hank almost choked on the saliva pooled in his mouth and covered up his blushing with another round of deep-lung coughing. He glanced left and right with determined movements, playing like they were in a scene of the *Mission: Impossible* television show. "Oh, definitely hard. No one worth a damn likes soft tacos, love." Hank held his breath, knowing being that forthright could go either way—and fast.

Floyd placed three fingertips against his lips to stifle a laugh. "You're so bad. But I really gotta go so I can be back at the eatery by two o'clock. Last week, they goofed up the crab legs order, and I don't trust the high schoolers I have on shift today."

"Yeah, you don't want to be late for that ass-whoopin' in the park."

"If only he'd play me in checkers, I'd send him running home, crying for his mommy."

Hank laughed and waved Floyd off. "Oh, you. Get outta here, love. Don't be a stranger."

Floyd left the Taco Shed, and Hank watched his next-door business owner drive away until his early afternoon shift manager blocked his view and entered through the door.

"G'morning, Mr. Steel. Everything okay from last night?"

Hank forced the smutty images of the Castaway's owner from his head. "Yeah. Wait. Why do you ask? Did something happen, Joel?"

"A fistfight broke out in here last night."

"A *what*? And no one thought to call me? And how do you know and I don't? You didn't work last night."

"I was here, eating. On a date."

"Follow me to the office. Tell me what happened." Hank turned for the back room and maneuvered through the tables with Joel in tow, the spurs on Hank's rattlesnake boots clacking against the wooden floor.

"Some high school seniors from the football team had pushed, like, four tables together so they could all sit together. But a group of freshmen were already sitting at one of those tables."

Hank stopped and faced Joel. "Let me guess. The food was dumped on the floor, and one of the freshmen thought he'd be big and bad and try to impress someone by standing up to the seniors."

Joel scrunched his face. "How'd ya know?"

"I was a teenager once too, contrary to popular belief." Hank continued onward to his office, the clacking of his boots accentuating every step.

"So, everyone faced off, and when the seniors realized they had an audience, they were relentless. Some punches were thrown. Some tables were flipped. A chair was tossed into the grill area."

"Police called?"

"*Nah*, we got in between them and stressed how it was in the seniors' best interests if they left *before* we called the cops. I helped sweep up."

"You missed an onion."

"Excuse me, sir?"

Hank chuckled and took a few moments to catch his breath. "Nothin'. I'm just playin' with ya, love."

Joel reached for his Taco Shed cooking apron as Hank deviated into his office, leaving the door open.

"I'm not sticking around long, Joel. Do you need anything else from me?"

Joel poked his head into the doorway as he tied the apron behind his neck. "You gonna try to catch Mr. Floyd's chess games?"

"What do you know about that, love?"

"Oh, c'mon, Mr. Steel. It's no secret you have the hots for him. I think it's cute. We all think you should say something to him. You've been ogling him for years now."

Hank leaned forward just enough to swing the door shut as Joel continued to talk. When the door clicked in the latch, Hank yelled through it, "Stick to making tacos and not playing matchmaker!"

He heard Joel laugh from the other side of the door and then walk away.

7: WORM IN A DOG'S HEART

Stepp shambled forward into the throne room, revealing himself.

Anya sneered. "Well, well. Look what the cat dragged in. I don't remember inviting you back here."

Stepp whimpered and cowered in the corner.

"Don't you have a new master to fuck over? I should have the vultures rip you apart right now."

Stepp nodded and reached his hands to her, pleading.

"You *want* permanent death?"

He nodded with more gusto.

"Ha! You don't deserve permanent death. What you did to me—what you *stole* from me—you only deserve to be the lowest of the low, to serve the bottom-feeders forever. You are nothing but a worm in a dog's heart, and I curse you to live for all eternity in this decrepit, imbecilic state." Anya spit in Stepp's direction, the growled, "Get him out of my sight and back to his rightful owner."

The vultures took flight in a counterclockwise tornado and exited with Stepp through the doorway from which he had entered.

"Think that's the last we'll see of him?" Melissa asked.

"Probably not."

"You gonna leave that there?" She gestured to the voodoo doll on the throne.

"Yep. It's a good reminder to the girls that even a smaller version of me can kick their ass. You ready to go?"

"I can't just stay in here forever?" Melissa joked.

"Afraid it doesn't work like that. Don't worry. I'll drop you off literally on his doorstep."

"He's probably at work."

Anya nodded. "Have you contemplated what you'll tell Hank if he asks how you got here so quickly?"

"Well …" Melissa ran some quick calculations through her head. "Nope. I got nothin'. I can't use the hitchhiking route, as I would need another two or three days to make it line up. You sure we can't just hunker down here for a few days to make it believable?"

"No can do. I'm concerned that, even in the short amount of time you've been here already, things are taking effect."

"What exactly would happen to me?"

"The netherworld isn't designed for a full-blood human. Did you see that movie *Gremlins* that came out this summer?"

"*Umm*, yeah."

"Remember what happened to the gremlin in the microwave?"

"Wait. You mean, *you* saw *Gremlins*?"

"What? Do you think I spend all my time flying around and doing evil witch stuff? I'm still a person. I have a high respect for all the arts. Except *Grease 2*." Anya visibly shivered. "Still don't know what that abomination was about. Anyway … gremlin, microwave. You get the visual."

"I guess I could hang around Vegas for a few days first, then head to his shop. So, change of landing location. There's a park near him. Lots of places to hide and to sleep undetected."

"That'll work." Anya put her chin to her chest, letting the black veil fall forward over her pale face, and plumes of purple consuming them replaced the throne room.

Melissa felt like she was falling while inside a dream, but she couldn't startle herself awake. Then she noted a mixture of sand and grass under her fingers. She opened her eyes; she was on all fours on the outskirts of a large park. To her immediate left were a handful of rows of chess tables, all occupied. She stood and beheld the scenery.

She watched an elderly man walk past her, not acknowledging her or the witch, afterward sitting across from a young male at a chess table.

"Popular spot."

"It's beautiful," Melissa said. "I could stay here for a few days, no problem."

"Good. I'll leave ya to it then."

Melissa turned to face the witch. "Wait. Where are you going?"

"You think I'm letting Baron off that easily? I can't let him have a moment's rest."

"A witch's work is never done, huh?"

Anya wagged a finger at Melissa. "You know what? You just gave me an idea."

"*Great.*" Melissa rolled her eyes. "Me and my big mouth."

"You have a few nights to kill …"

Melissa raised her eyebrows, waiting for Anya to finish her sentence.

Anya sighed long and hard. "You have a few nights to … *kill*. God, you are dense, child."

"You mean, while I'm here, I—"

"You wanted to be Stepp's replacement. You wanted to be the Mushroom Cult leader. Here's a perfect time to put your money where your mouth is. Add to my army of ghouls over the next few nights, and you'll be well on your way to earning my trust and to unlocking some of the deeper-rooted spells in the book. The ones that will bring you closer to my state of being—closer to replacing me on my throne when I become divine."

Melissa felt her stomach explode with flutters, and her adrenaline burst like a dam through her veins. "How do I even start? I mean, who do I look for? Where do I go?"

"This isn't a job where I hold your hand. You need to figure it out yourself."

Melissa spaced out, deep in thought, as she seemed to look at the elderly man and the young boy engaged in a chess game. A movement to her left distracted the movie playing in her head, and she darted her gaze to the newcomer at the chess table. "Oh, shit." Melissa backpedaled deeper into the thicket surrounding the park.

Anya ducked and moved alongside the girl. "What?"

"It's Uncle Hank. He's talking to the old dude and the kid at the chess table. Fuck!"

Anya giggled.

"What's so funny?" Melissa whispered forcefully.

"The irony is beautiful."

Melissa shushed her and focused on Hank. She watched him throw back his head when he laughed and place a hand on the elderly man's shoulder. She squinted to see better, as realization dawned on her. "I think Uncle Hank likes that guy." Melissa watched him pull a chair to the chess table and lean back, relaxed, like he had always belonged there. "He was with this guy, Olli, for years. But Olli disappeared, and we never knew what happened to him. Uncle Hank refuses to talk about it. Olli was a cop or something back in the day."

"Maybe he's in the Vertigo Motel, with the rest of the skeletons in the closets."

"The what?" Melissa eyed the witch.

"One day, child. One day I'll take you there so you can see what everyone spends their lives hiding from everyone else. But you're not quite ready for the Vertigo just yet." Anya snapped and pointed at Melissa. "I got it!"

"Got what?"

"I know how we'll get you to Hank without raising too much suspicion."

"I'm all ears."

"Let me brainstorm the idea a little more before I tell you. I'd say, you only need to be out here for about forty-eight hours, for what I have in mind to sound feasible."

"I can do two days."

"I know you can. Now stay inconspicuous. You don't want to end up like Sandy."

Melissa eyed the witch. "Who's Sandy?"

"The dog from *Annie*."

Melissa rolled her eyes and focused on Hank again. "You gotta get a hobby. Oh, what area around here would be best to hunt for victims?" She turned to look at Anya, but the witch was gone. "Figures."

Melissa settled on her haunches and watched Hank interact with the elderly man as the chess game progressed. Hank seemed to force laughter at things that probably weren't that funny, and he would occasionally pat the man's arm or knee but quickly removed it, as if it would burn should he let it linger too long. Melissa chuckled and shook her head. "Make your move, Uncle Hank," she mumbled to her herself. "You deserve it."

It appeared the young boy had won the game—Melissa couldn't be sure, as she had no idea how the game was played or what the pieces represented—because the elderly man shook his head and proffered his hand across the board. The boy shook it and rose to his feet.

Melissa let her backpack slide to the ground. She unzipped it and rummaged through its contents. She frantically moved items from side to side as she realized the book was missing. *Bitch took the book!* Her fingers felt the cold metal of her dad's gun.

She contemplated how easy it would be to add to the Mushroom Cult tonight, now that she remembered she had grabbed the firearm.

SALEM, MASSACHUSETTS; 1984

8: WE AREN'T THE WORLD

Madam Hapney locked the door to her shop, returned to her desk, and ran her finger through the charred section, recalling how effortlessly Melissa had set the wood ablaze. Going to the police had now only seemed to have done more harm than good. The girl was missing and probably angrier than she had been when she had confronted Hapney in her shop.

"Bridgett ..." a man called out behind her.

She startled as she turned toward the sound. "Oh, Baron. Don't do that to me." She placed a hand over her heart and sighed.

Baron walked around her desk and ran his tongue across the top row of his teeth as he surveyed the arson damage. "It's worse than we thought."

"Oh?" Hapney asked, tidying her stack of *Psychic Today & Tomorrow* magazines on the side table.

"Our witch brought the girl into the netherworld. Looks like she's priming her well. She has a lot to learn, but she's come a long way in a short amount of time."

"I told you. I've been working with Melissa for months, with very little progress. Anya gets her hooks in the girl, and she's setting fire to things."

"They're in Vegas right now."

"Anya chanced transporting a full mortal?" Hapney eyed Baron, hoping she had heard him wrong.

"Looks like she either doesn't care what happens to Melissa or has so much blind faith in the girl's powers that she doesn't think it will affect her."

"Reckless. Teenager or not, she's just a girl."

"Halfway corrupted too." Baron tapped his index finger against his lips. "We gotta go to them. Waiting for them to come to us is futile. And we'll lose precious time."

"You want *my* help? I can't compare or stand up to Anya's arts. I'm just a humble psychic, trying to make ends meet in the witchcraft capital of the world. Facing Anya is way beyond anything in my wheelhouse."

"Why do you constantly doubt yourself, Bridgett? You are pure of heart, and your intentions are true. Don't you think that holds some weight against the darkness we are facing? I wouldn't be coming to you if I thought you would be a hindrance."

Hapney blushed. "But we aren't the world. There are many others who are more powerful than me, who would chomp at the bit to dig their claws into Anya. Can't you recruit them instead?"

"Could? Yes. Want to? No. Melissa knows you personally. She doesn't know anyone else who might want to join the crusade. That makes you special. That provides a chance where you could get through to her."

"She set fire to my shop the last time we were face to face!" Hapney angrily and desperately pointed at the charred desk. "I would think having me there would be a handicap and not an asset."

"I think you underestimate the heart of a teenager. She is impressionable. That's how Anya got to her. That's how you'll get her back."

Hapney sighed and closed her eyes. Images of the day Melissa had visited her shop danced behind Hapney's eyelids. Melissa had been an innocent and pure, young girl full of promise and gusto. "Fine," Hapney whispered and opened her eyes. "But is it safe for you to take me through the netherworld to get there?"

"Who said I'd put your safety in jeopardy like that?" Baron smiled and flashed two plane tickets. "We leave tomorrow morning, first flight out of Logan."

"You know what you are?" Hapney asked, smirking.

"A genius?"

"Conniving!"

Baron chuckled and massaged Hapney's shoulders. "We'll prevail. I just know it."

Madam Hapney pursed her lips and took a final look at her scorched desk before she nodded in agreement.

LAS VEGAS, NEVADA; 1984

9: BEATING A DEAD HORSE
TO DEATH … AGAIN

Melissa huffed and situated her backpack farther on her shoulder as she turned down an alleyway. The top curvature of the sun had finally disappeared behind the horizon of buildings and the desert beyond. Shadows grew longer and wider as lights from the nightlife grew brighter, beckoning the adventurous.

She swallowed hard as she passed a brick wall graffitied with slang and cuss words—and a few phone numbers, advertising a good time. A newspaper blew across the small alley, its pages flapping like wings, before it struck the concrete, then skidded like a hockey puck against a blue dumpster. She contemplated finding a corner to remove her dad's gun from the backpack so she could tuck it into her waistband for protection, but the thought of stopping for even a moment before she reached a well-populated area sent shivers down her spine.

She figured she might need to wait until the sun was completely set and darkness blanketed the streets before anyone worthy of sacrifice to the cult would reveal themselves for their nightly services. Melissa really wasn't even sure how to tell a street walker from a pedestrian.

Hookers didn't have a sign around their necks, advertising their intents, did they? Would the girls look like the stereotypical prostitutes from the movies, where they wore ripped fishnets, vixen-red lipstick, teased hair, and leather miniskirts? Or was real life a little more discreet and subtle? What if Melissa killed someone innocent?

Without having a specific direction, Melissa turned right into an alleyway that mirrored the one she had just left. She passed two men huddled around a large barrel, with flames licking from its opened top.

"Gets cold at night, girlie. You want to cuddle with us against the fire?"

Melissa stopped and turned to the two men.

One of them flashed a toothless grin. "There's plenty a' room." He slid over to create space between him and his friend.

"I think I'm all set," she said and moved onward.

At the end of the alley, she turned left toward the shine of neon lights. When she emerged onto what seemed to be a main drag, the flashing amber lights of the Golden Mirage Casino blinded her for a moment. She stopped and beheld the glitz and the glamor of the traffic and the patrons. She ogled at the women in their long flowing gowns, adorned with what looked like specks from disco balls when the lights hit them. Colors of turquoise and sea-foam green and yellow moved with the high heels and the flawless hairdos. Men in tuxedos and top hats slipped chauffeurs and valets rolls of bills.

Melissa admired the array of cars that slowed as they passed the Golden Mirage. Flashy sports cars with loud exhausts, pristine luxury cars from the sixties, and a Rolls Royce circled, waiting for a turn to enter the valet port. Limousines stopped out front to let their passengers disembark.

Melissa decided to cross the street toward the dazzling show of well-to-do fashion, and when her foot stepped off the curb, a car beeped at her. She startled and stepped backward as a stainless-steel car slowly rolled past her, looking more like a time machine from outer space than a car.

Stunned both by almost getting hit and the car's unique appearance, she kept her gaze glued to the coupe as it made a U-turn in the middle of the street, stopped in front of the casino's entrance, and both doors opened, going straight into the air instead of swinging outward.

A man stepped out, plopped a fedora with a red feather onto his head, and pushed down on the door to close it. A valet helped his passenger—a woman wearing copper-colored glasses that looked more like swimming goggles—from the car, and they disappeared into the casino's lobby, leaving the passenger door up, like a gull with a wing permanently raised skyward.

Gawking at the futuristic-looking vehicle across the street, Melissa had let down her guard and had momentarily forgotten about the potential dangers from the alleyways behind her ... until she was shoved into the street, her torso twisting around from the force of someone yanking her backpack off her shoulders. She clawed at the strap, frantic to not let her possessions get stolen—mostly because of the gun—but the momentum of stumbling backward was too great, and the strap slipped to her wrists and right through her fingers with ease.

A figure in a hooded sweatshirt turned on his heels and bolted back into the shadows of the alley.

"Hey! Thief!" she yelled, as she had seen in movies when women get their purses snatched in parks, hoping someone from the busy street would help. She needed to act fast—either keep yelling and wait for help or make pursuit. She glanced across the street and realized not a single soul had so much as flinched at her first call for help.

She focused on the figure vanishing into the shadows, her bookbag tucked under his armpit.

She gritted her teeth, dug her soles into the blacktop, and sprinted after him. Her knees and stomach felt each pound of her feet against the pavement as she rounded the corner, deeper into the maze of alleys. She caught a glimpse of the thief ahead as he leaped for a fire escape and climbed the metal ladder.

She stopped underneath the bottom rung, which dangled a few feet above her head, and jumped for it. Her fingertips grazed the metal bar but slipped off. She jumped again to the same result. She heard the vibration traveling downward through the metal as the thief climbed higher, farther away from her. She was losing him.

She backpedaled and looked up the side of the building just in time to see him dip into an open window on the fourth floor. She balled her fists and headed for the side door to the building. The door was unlocked, and she thought she had ripped it from its hinges with the force she had applied to open it, from both the adrenaline and the fear coursing through her.

She lunged into the hallway, the odor of urine and stale alcohol assaulting her nose.

Melissa noticed a staircase to the side of the hallway and bounded up the steps three at a time. She counted each landing, estimating when she had reached the fourth floor. She shoved through the fire door and found herself in a hallway with a squishy, stained red carpet. She didn't have a plan now that she had reached the floor where she had seen the thief go.

Melissa slowly traversed the hallway, stopping at each apartment door to listen for any sounds that might tip her off about the thief's location. She wasn't sure what exactly she was listening for; did purse snatchers make a distinct sound? She hovered her ear in front of the second door and strained to hear anything from inside. She caught a television playing an action movie with a lot of gunshots. She moved on to the next apartment and leaned her ear toward the door.

The knob turned, and the door swung inward.

Melissa stumbled into the middle of the hallway and instinctively looked at the floor, embarrassed at being caught. From the corner of her eye, she spied a broad-shouldered male standing motionless in the doorframe. She was afraid to make eye contact with him, but she was equally planted to the floor.

The man stepped into the hallway but stopped next to her. "What do we have here?"

Melissa gulped and tilted her head to see him better.

"Can I help you with something? Have you come to apply?" He circled her slowly, scrutinizing her with his eyes. "You'd need to ditch those clothes, but I'm sure one of the other girls would have something you could borrow until you got your own. And your hair. That won't do either."

Melissa felt the blood rush to her hands, and her body tingled in fear and nausea.

The man clicked his tongue against his teeth and stood straight. "You can start tonight. The strip is just getting hoppin', so you shouldn't waste any time, or you'll just have the drunken sloppy scraps to pick from. I get eighty percent for the first six months, and, if we're a good fit, then I lower my take to fifty percent." He lifted her chin with two fingers and forced her to look at him. "You only answer to me, understand? Name's Mustang Mack."

Melissa swatted Mack's hand off her chin. "I'm not a whore!" She turned to run the way she had come. She concentrated on the fire door leading to the stairwell and hoped Mustang Mack wasn't chasing after her.

"Run fast, little bunny!" Mack called after her, and his laugh sounded like rolling thunder. "Out here, we're all *whores*!"

The fire door clicked closed as Melissa hit the first landing on the way down, and she could still hear Mustang Mack's bellowing chuckle from above. Her hands didn't stop shaking until she hit ground level, striding back toward the main strip.

She focused on the flashing lights and the hubbub ahead of her, while she felt a pit in her stomach over the lost backpack and weapon. Relief engulfed her when she remembered Anya had reclaimed the Mushroom Cult Book; at least the thief didn't have his grubby hands on that too.

The street sprawled left and right, giving her an insight into how large the world could be. But she realized she couldn't hunt anymore tonight; her search for her first victim would have to be paused until she could figure out how to replace the murder weapon.

She tucked her chin to her chest, galloped across the street, and let herself be bathed in the neon lights and flashing bulbs.

"Hey, kid!" a doorman in a tuxedo yelled. "Are you lost?"

She debated whether to stop and answer. While she was lost and had nowhere to stay or to sleep for the next thirty-six hours, she couldn't risk an interrogation and a phone call to the police. She also didn't want to raise suspicion by fleeing from him. "Just taking a shortcut back to the hotel! Family's on vacation. Thanks for looking out!"

He nodded and immediately forgot about her as he held open the door for a pair of ladies who looked like they had stepped out of a 1920s' crime-noir novel.

She quickened her pace down the strip, more to distance herself from Mustang Mack than to escape the judging gazes from the debutantes and Rockefellers crowding the sidewalk. She shoved her hands into her pocket and slumped her shoulders forward, trying to create more of a barrier around her face.

She began to come to terms with the fact that tonight would just be a bust, and she would have to regroup tomorrow for her first kill and sacrifice to the cult. Now she had to figure out what to do with herself for the rest of the night—both to keep safe and out of sight from patrolmen.

Without any kind of protection, she was leery about sleeping anywhere near this location. Both the strip, with its constant entertainment, and the alleyways, with their dark insidiousness, seemed equally dangerous and unwise choices. Remembering the outskirts of the park from earlier in the day, she realized hiding in the outlining shrubbery would be the safest bet. Now she had to remember how to get back there in the dark.

She came to an intersection as the lights and the sounds of the strip faded behind her. Getting her bearings and a sense of direction, her intuition felt the park was straight ahead. She looked both ways and trotted across the street, leaving the row of casinos behind her, entering rows of bungalows.

Some had collapsed front porches. Some had caved-in roofs, and some were altogether dilapidated and crumbling. The graffiti became more frequent again as the streetlights grew farther apart. Shadows seemed to dance on their own, and the breeze was the loudest sound she heard over her sneakers crunching the broken concrete sidewalk. She started to think maybe leaving the safety of the razzle and dazzle of the strip was a bad idea.

She halted when she saw a small flame flicker to life in the darkness to her left, hover in midair for a moment until it rose slightly, and lit the end of a cigarette. The glow illuminated the shape of a smaller figure leaning against a tree, halfway down a driveway containing a broken-down jalopy.

"Tourist off the beaten path, *eh*?" the young woman said as she pushed herself off the tree. The glowing cigarette bounced closer to Melissa, almost as if nothing were holding it, until the owner of the voice graced the outskirts of the reach from the streetlight.

"Something like that." Melissa regarded the girl suspiciously.

The girl exhaled a puff of white smoke and scanned Melissa from head to toe. "*Nah*. You a runaway."

Melissa stepped backward and chortled. "I am *not*! My family is staying at the … the … the Golden Mirage!"

The girl clapped her hands together once. "*Bah*! You're a runaway and a terrible liar. The Golden Mirage is a casino, not a hotel. So, if your family is staying there, it's because the mob has them tied up in the basement."

Melissa scratched a nonexistent itch on her side from nervousness and murmured, "I just want a place to sleep."

"What's that?" The girl stepped forward.

Melissa took a deep breath and surveyed the person standing in front of her. The girl looked no more than in her late teens. Her clothes were older and threadbare but not stained and dirty. Her makeup was heavy but not obscene. Melissa wrestled with what to say next.

"Name's Laura." The girl tucked the cigarette behind her back to not accidentally burn Melissa and proffered her other hand.

"Mel." She shook the girl's hand, then stepped back quickly—just in case.

"I won't bite."

Melissa kicked a pebble into the front lawn of the house they stood in front of. "Sorry. Didn't mean to be rude. I've had a shit night. Someone robbed me of my backpack."

"Animals. That's what they are. I'm guessing you had everything you ran away with in there, right?"

Melissa nodded, not willing to divulge the inventory she had lost.

"Has happened to all of us at one point or another. You choose to live on the streets, you gotta be prepared for the streets to rob you of everything at some point."

"Are you ... homeless?" Melissa wasn't sure if that term was insulting, but she didn't know how else to ask.

"None of us are truly homeless. The streets are my home. I'd say all these people"—she waved her arms around, gesturing to the rows of suburbia—"suffer from being *overhomed*."

"*Overhomed*." Melissa chuckled. "I like it."

"Where are you staying?"

"I didn't have a solid plan yet, but I was thinking of that park with all the chess tables."

"You mean, Tribulation?"

"The park's called Tribulation?" Melissa eyed her warily.

Laura snickered. "Well, that's not it's real name. It's just what us outcasts call it, like a street nickname. But if you want to take a chance out there, alone and without supplies, be my guest." She dropped her cigarette to the ground and mashed it under her threadbare sneakers. "See ya 'round, Mel."

"Wait!"

Laura stopped her about-face and smirked without looking at Melissa.

"Do you have a place to stay tonight? Or could I just hang with you? I only need a place to stay tonight and tomorrow night, until I can go to my uncle's house. Well, he's not my biological uncle. He's my grandpapa's best friend and has been in my life since …" Thoughts of what she had done to her grandfather just twenty-four hours ago struck her hard. Her stomach felt empty, and her heart rate quickened as her conscience took over.

"No need to explain. I think I can hook you up. It'll cost ya though."

"I don't have any money, and I told you all my stuff was stolen."

"I don't mean by money. Tomorrow night, I'll show you."

Melissa furrowed her brows and contemplated the risks to the benefits. "Okay, deal."

"Come on. I know a place where we can stay up ahead. You might have to share the floor with some roaches, but a roof will be over your head, and your safety is guaranteed." Laura looped her arm through Melissa's and led her away from the driveway where they stood.

Melissa glanced back at the dark house. "What were you doing in that person's yard?"

"Finishing a job."

"A ... job?"

"Us deviants have to do something to keep food in our bellies and to keep the violence from targeting us."

"I assume this job wasn't anything ..." Mel trailed off, again not wanting to insult her gracious host.

"Legal? If everything I did was legal, I wouldn't be free out here."

Melissa nodded.

"So, who's this not-uncle you're meeting? And why do you need to wait?"

"Long story."

"It's a long walk."

"Why are you being so nice to me?"

"These streets would chew you up and spit you out before morning."

"I don't think you know—"

"How long did it take for someone to gank your shit?" Laura stopped and glared at Melissa. "Don't be all cocky out here, princess. You will get fucked." She eyed Melissa up and down. "You'd either get raped or beaten before sunrise, so watch your *P*s and *Q*s with the only person you can trust out here."

"Sorry. I-I just wasn't ready for what happened to me."

"We all get robbed. It's what you do afterward that matters."

But Melissa wasn't thinking about her backpack; her thoughts had created a montage of images, speeding through the events of the last week, from Stepp's office to her bedroom.

"Anyone else bother you besides your mugger?"

Melissa chuckled while wiping a single tear that had formed in the corner of her eye. "Yeah, an upstanding gentleman named Mustang Mack."

Laura didn't respond right away. They passed a few houses before she spoke. "I hope you didn't agree to anything."

"Nah, he thought I was looking for a job."

"He thinks everyone wants to fuck for him."

"Disgusting."

"Yeah, he is."

Melissa eyed Laura. "I meant whores in general. The whole thing. Having sex for cash. Scum."

Laura pointed a finger at Melissa's chest. "Before you go passing judgment, just make sure you are lily white yourself, princess." She huffed and stormed forward.

"I-I didn't mean to make you mad. Wait up." Melissa broke into a powerwalk to catch up to Laura. "I'm sorry, okay?"

"Look." Laura stopped again and spun to face Melissa. "Sometimes, out here, we do things we need to do in order to survive. Shoplifting, robbing, stealing cars, killin'—and yes, sometimes even hooking—isn't beneath the best of us. So take your hoity-toity lil' behind back to whatever resort your fuckin' uncle is staying at, and leave the streets to the people who run them. You're out of your league here, princess." Laura spun and strode onward.

"Hold up! Hold up!" Melissa grabbed her elbow. "I'm sorry, okay? This is all new to me." Melissa closed her eyes and took a deep inhale. "I'm on the run because ... because ... well ..."

Laura folded her arms and tapped her foot. "Spit it out, chickadee."

"Back where I'm from, I—" The sound of a branch crunching high on a tree near them and the flash of a black mass distracted her from her confession for a moment. She studied Laura's face to see if she had noticed it to.

When Laura's lips remained pursed, her face scrunched, and her foot tapping, Melissa realized Laura had not seen the vulture land on the branch. Melissa glanced at the bird of prey, not moving her head, and noticed the vulture's beady eyes fixed on her face. She swallowed hard.

"I may have all night, but I'm getting fucking bored with you," Laura said.

"I killed two people."

The vulture hissed angrily and flapped its massive wings one time to take flight. The branch bounced like a rubber band.

Laura still had not noticed the bird, even in the commotion it had made while leaving. "Who'd you kill, princess? You pullin' my chain?"

A jalopy turned onto the street from ahead, and the two girls watched it roll to a stop beside them. The window rolled down, but the driver's face remained hidden in the darkness of the car. "Hey, girls. How much for both of you at the same time?"

"Get bent," Laura said and waved him off.

"Fuck you, whore!" came the reply from inside the car, and the engine revved unnecessarily loudly before the car peeled away in a screech.

"Compensating for how tiny your dick is?" Laura yelled at the car as it sped toward the strip.

"Oh, she'll do," Anya whispered in Melissa's ear, materializing next to her.

Melissa startled and glared at the witch. "Let me handle this, please," she said through gritted teeth so Laura wouldn't hear.

"She'll make a fine addition to the cult, don't ya think?"

"Get lost. She's helping me right now."

"Don't tell me that you're getting soft. It wouldn't behoove you to think of this piece of meat as nothing more than a smear on society. Get too close—too sympathetic—and you'll be useless to me."

Laura started walking again. "You were saying?"

Anya kept in step with Melissa. "I gotta hear this."

Melissa shushed the witch before answering. "I'm more of a badass than you think. I killed the girl my boyfriend was cheating on me with."

Anya chortled loudly. "Boyfriend. Good one. Nice cover."

"And I set fire to another bitch's desk, then killed my grandfather."

Laura burst into laughing. "I feel like you just described a scene from a movie you've seen. You didn't do any of those things, princess. Plus, aren't you here with your granddad's best friend? Your story has more holes than Swiss cheese." Laura shood her head and glared at Melissa. "Don't try to be something you're not out here. We'll see right through you, and then you'll be taken for a ride. Stay safe by staying honest."

Anya had now surrendered to a full-on belly laugh fit. "Oh, this is great. You actually confess the truth of these heinous crimes, and little miss scrumptious doesn't believe you for a moment. You really are pathetic. Can you do *anything* right, *princess*?"

Melissa swallowed her anger. If she wanted any chance at all to became as powerful as Anya promised, she knew she had to tolerate the barrage of insults—even if for just a little longer.

"C'mon." Laura grabbed Melissa's hand. "It's just the next block over."

Melissa broke into a trot to keep pace with Laura, who didn't slow down when they crossed the next main street without looking both ways. They faded into the shadows of the dim side street.

Laura stopped in front of a structure that resembled more of a shack than a home. "Remember. You may be my guest, but you're still the new girl. So act like one. Starr has even less tolerance for bullshit."

"Starr? Is that her real name?"

Laura shrugged. "Who knows. Never thought to ask. But she'd cut you just as fast as she'll hug you, so watch yourself."

"Noted." Melissa nodded.

Laura approached the front door and knocked two times fast, paused, then four times fast, paused again, then two times again. "That's how we know it's not the cops," she whispered to Melissa.

Two, four, two, Melissa repeated in her head, in case she needed to use this shack as a haven later.

The door creaked open to reveal a woman much older than Melissa had expected to see. She didn't know why she had thought Starr would be another teenager—other than her name maybe—but the sight of a middle-aged woman surprised her.

"Starr, this is Melissa. She's new in town and needs a place to crash for a few nights."

"Two nights, ma'am," Melissa clarified.

"Pah! *Ma'am?* Oh, little one. Come in. Come in." Starr stepped aside to clear the front entrance.

Melissa followed Laura inside and scanned the two-room shack.

Laura plopped onto a sleeping bag already unrolled on the floor. "Safest place in Vegas for us working girls."

"Oh, you!" Starr said and flapped her hand once at Laura. "Are you hungry, Melissa?"

"No, ma'am."

Starr studied Melissa's face. "*Hmm.* I guess it's hard to eat when your stomach is doing flippity-flops of uncertainty and you're trying to figure out if what you've done makes you a bad person or if you are a good person just doing bad things." Starr closed one eye and glared harder. "You have a dark, dark cloud over your head, little one."

"*Fucksticks!* You were telling the truth!" Laura slapped her thigh. "She was telling me about all these people she killed, but I didn't believe—"

"*Zsa, zsa, zsa!* Shh! Give me a minute of quiet. Let me see …" Starr brushed Melissa's hair behind her ear and leaned in, like a doctor doing an eye exam.

Anya appeared behind Starr—her upper body to one side so Melissa could only see from her waist up—and stuck her thumbs in both ears and twisted them while crossing her eyes.

Melissa snorted a chuckle and put her hand to her mouth. "Sorry."

"Something funny?"

Melissa dared to spy Anya again; this time, the witch was doing a jig behind Starr while sticking two fingers above the back of her head in a bunny-ear taunt.

"I'm sorry, ma'am." It took all she had to stifle another laugh. "I laugh sometimes when I'm nervous."

Anya folded her arms away from her chest, squatted low, and did a Russian dance, kicking her feet in front of her while keeping her back straight.

Melissa closed her eyes to will away the witch and her antics. When she opened them, the pale priestess was gone, and Starr regarded Mel with a confused expression. "I'm better now, ma'am." Melissa forced her expression to become stoic.

"You have secrets." Starr turned from her and eyed Laura. "Where did you say you found her?"

"She had been mugged and was wandering past the strip."

"What was stolen?"

"I dunno. You gotta ask her."

Starr did not look at Melissa but asked, "What was stolen from you?"

"My backpack."

"What was in your backpack? Don't make me pull every piece of information from you."

Laura snickered from the floor.

"My dad's gun. Some school supplies. Odds and ends."

"The gun you used to kill—" Starr made eye contact with Melissa. "No, not the gun. The gun was supposed to be for self-defense. You used something else to kill. But ... But I can't quite see what it was."

"You little devil! Your street cred just went sky-high in my books, Mel. I thought I'd done some shitty things, but kill someone?" Laura made a high-five motion into the air.

A cockroach the size of a matchbox car scurried across the floor.

"You sure you ain't hungry?" Starr asked.

"Yes, ma'am. I just need a place to stay until I meet up with my uncle day after tomorrow."

"Her *uncle* is the best friend of her grandfather, who she knocked off."

Starr closed her eyes. "No, he's not dead. Not yet."

Melissa didn't know if it was relief or dread that engulfed her. "How can you know these things?"

Starr opened one eye. "We all have our talents. You, me, ... the black birds of prey."

Melissa stepped backward. "What do you know about the vultures?"

"What vultures?" Laura popped a wad of strawberry-flavored Bubble Yum into her mouth.

Starr turned her back to the girls and sauntered into the small makeshift kitchen. She filled a teapot with water from the faucet and put it over a small flame on the stovetop. "I see them, but I don't think they can see me. I'm not part of your war."

"Wait. War? What *war*?" Laura stood from the sleeping bag. "What the fuck is even going on in here? Who the hell are you? *Both* of you?" Her eyes darted between Melissa and Starr.

"It's not supposed to be a war," Melissa mumbled.

"Oh, little one, you can't have evil without good. I'm just a humble observer, but I can see who holds all the cards. My place will always be neutral—a paradise for sloths."

"Hey, I resemble that remark!" Laura snapped and laughed. "Why do I get the feeling we aren't talking about a war between the girls and the pimps?"

"Maybe we are," Starr answered and smirked at her. "But who are the girls, and who are the pimps?"

The teapot sailed across the room and splattered against the far wall.

Starr flexed her lips against her teeth and glared at Melissa. "Did you do that?"

Melissa, wide-eyed, stepped backward and shook her head.

Anya, clinging like a spider to the ceiling above their head, called down, "This one's a real winner."

Melissa looked up at the witch, and Starr followed her gaze. "What's up there?"

"She can't see me," Anya said. "None of these halfwits can. She talks a good game, may have just enough insight to *sense* things, but she's not powerful enough to see me. Unless I want her to."

"Then how can she see the vultures?" Melissa asked in a normal tone.

"Who are you talking to?" Starr scampered from the room and stopped next to Laura's sleeping bag to peer at the kitchen ceiling again from a safe distance.

"Anyone can see those twerps if they want them to," Anya answered. "Plus, she's just eaten a handful of shrooms. She'll believe anything you say right now."

Melissa turned her attention from the spider-witch on the ceiling and watched Laura collecting the teapot from the ground. "Talking to? No one. What made you think I was talking to anyone?"

Starr wagged a finger at the ceiling. "You were talking to something on the ceiling."

"You were," Laura said. "She might be all doped up, but I'm straight as an arrow right now."

"God. I sometimes ask God for advice."

Laura nodded, accepting the explanation.

Starr rubbed her eyes and watched Laura, still on her hands and knees, clean up the spill. "Thank you. How did that get over there anyway?"

"You slapped it across the room when you turned around," Melissa said.

"I can be so clumsy sometimes."

Laura glared at Melissa with a knowing look.

"Are you done working for the night?" Starr asked Laura.

"Yeah, I don't think I can handle any more excitement tonight. I'll give Mack his cut tomorrow."

Melissa heard her heart hammer in her ears. "You work for Mack?"

"I work for myself! But I toss Mack a few bucks every few days so he stays off my back and leaves me be."

Fucking whore, Melissa thought and felt her skin crawl for being in such close proximity to the exact filth she had vowed to eradicate.

"I'm tuckered out," Starr said. "We should get some shut-eye. Melissa, you can sleep on the recliner."

Melissa surveyed the shopworn blue recliner at the foot of Starr's bed.

"It doesn't recline anymore, but it's more comfortable than the floor," Starr added.

"Thank you, ma'am." Melissa shuffled past the sleeping bag and sat in the lumpy recliner. She pressed her hands together like she was praying, to create a pillow. She didn't want her face touching the fabric. "I won't bother you tomorrow. I'll leave in the morning."

"You're more than welcome to stay for as long as you need."

"Paradise for sloths," Melissa repeated and chuckled.

"Goodnight, princess," Laura said, slipping into the sleeping bag. "Glad I met you and saved you from the animals on the streets. It was like fate."

Melissa sighed heavily, her conscience weighing on her as to how she really felt about the girl keeping her safe.

10: THE ALCHEMY'S IN BLOOM

Hank Steel waited in his car, parked in the lot that his taco shop and Castaway's Eatery shared. He had to make it look as natural as possible when Floyd arrived to open his restaurant that Hank wasn't waiting for him. So Hank repeatedly collected a stack of papers, then messed them up, then collected them again.

He recognized the hum of the engine from Floyd's car and ensured he looked twice as busy for when Floyd drove past. He wanted to time it perfectly, both exiting their cars together, so a conversation didn't feel planned or forced.

When he heard the engine cut off, Hank swung open his car door and stalled a few more seconds to collect a pile of papers that had nothing to do with anything. He slid from the front seat, stifled another round of hacking coughs as best he could, and made eye contact with his business neighbor. "Morning."

"Hiya, Hank. Sorry I don't have a coffee for ya this morning."

Hank tried to chuckle in a nonobvious flirtatious way.

Floyd stepped toward the front doors of Castaway's, then stopped and turned. "Say, Hank, I have some contractors coming to the store tomorrow to measure out adding a side dining room."

"Business that good, huh?"

"It's boomin'. In fact, if it keeps up like this, I might make you an offer to buy out your side of the building."

"And who says my business isn't booming?" Hank asked with a coy smile.

"I'm joshing with ya. Anyway, just letting you know, in case you wanted to stop in to give your unbiased opinion of their plans. Sometimes it's hard for me to see the forest for the trees, ya know? Might be nice to have a neutral party there to tell me if their plans are shit or gold."

"I'm flattered, but I'd hate for you to take my advice and then go belly-up because it was a bad business move."

Floyd grinned. "Then if I go belly-up, it was never meant to be in the first place, and I'll just come begging you for a job. I can cook a pretty scrumptious taco!"

"Alright, alright. You twisted my arm. Just come by and grab me when they're here. I plan to be at the shop all day tomorrow. Got end-of-year bookkeeping I want to get a jump on."

"Got any plans for Christmas?"

"Same as every year. Watch *A Christmas Carol* and put a little too much whiskey in my hot cocoa until the day passes in a blur."

Floyd clamped an open palm to his chest. "You're killing me! That's the saddest thing I've ever heard."

"Never been one for holiday cheer, love." Hank almost didn't finish the sentence, as his lungs heaved, and he fought to take a breath.

"Well, you are more than welcome to spend Christmas with me and the family."

"Much obliged. I'll have to seriously consider that." Hank tried to keep his heart from hammering through his chest and his face from blushing the color of violet.

"Until tomorrow?"

"Until tomorrow. Have a nice day, Floyd." Hank headed for his Taco Shed without waiting for a reply. He didn't want any further chitchat to spoil the elation he felt.

11: WAR PARTY

Melissa slowly backed away from the bungalow's main room and eased the front door closed as quietly as she could so she wouldn't wake the sleeping Laura or Starr. When she felt the door shut with a *click* and confirmed neither woman had woken from her leaving, Melissa shoved her hands into her pants pockets and shivered from the chilly Vegas morning air. She scanned left and right, noticing how quiet—almost dead—the street felt. She hoped she was the only one awake and could escape the neighborhood unseen.

Melissa padded toward the main street again. Without any money or her personal supplies, she realized she would have to shoplift food, drinks, and any items she'd need to prove her worth to Anya tonight—even if she could only add one new cult member.

The glitz and glamor from last night had been replaced with normality and genericism on the strip, as the flashy cars had now given way to mundane daily drivers. She chose to go in the opposite direction of the casinos, trying her hand at finding a supermarket or a general store. She focused on the beat of her soles as she took each step while creating a mental list of what items she would need to snatch. She shook her head as she walked, realizing she couldn't shoplift anything as effective as another gun. If only she hadn't been mugged and her backpack stolen …

The lights from a convenience store's sign became visible over the low treetops, and Melissa quickened her pace. There might not be weapons in there but at least she could fill her belly before brainstorming her next errand.

A small bell chimed above the door when she pushed through, and a rotund man glanced up at her from behind the counter. He grunted and returned his focus to the morning newspaper sprawled in front of him.

Melissa surveyed the store's layout and the number of customers. The aisles were in perfect rows, and she was the only shopper as far as she could ascertain. She started in the aisle farthest from the counter and farthest from the cashier's line of sight. She scanned the snack items, calculating in her head the size of the food packages against the size of her pockets. She couldn't walk out with bulges that hadn't been there when she had entered. Her gaze swept over the bags of chips until she got to small packages of nuts and candy. Not the healthiest diet for the day, but it would have to do.

She turned her back to the front of the store to create a shield from her activity and hastily snatched a handful of bags of nuts from their hooks and jammed them into her back pockets.

A door directly in front of her swung open, and out came a middle-aged woman steering her small child by the shoulders. They stopped and made eye contact with Melissa as the restroom door swung closed behind them, clearly judging what they saw her do.

Melissa's heart thumped hard, and she turned on her heels and bolted for the front door. She placed her palms over her back pockets to keep the stolen snacks from bouncing out while she sprinted across the store.

"Hey!" the cashier yelled and stood as she streaked past him. "Get back here!"

Melissa hit the glass front door without slowing, thinking she had ripped it from its hinges, and bolted across the parking lot. She chanced a glance behind her and slowed her escape when she realized no one had taken up chase. She giggled when she thought to herself how the man behind the counter was too chubby to chase a runaway Skittle, even if he wanted to.

She found a small cut-through path separating the main strip from another area, and she thought it would be safest to get off the main road in case the cashier had called the police. The path gave way to a small strip mall; some stores were already open, while others were still blacked out.

Melissa quickly went through a mental Rolodex of murder weapons she could easily steal, trying to find the right one—ax, *too messy*; hammer, *too much force needed*; poison, *too slow*; machete, … *yes!*

She could swipe a kitchen knife or pocketknife from any department store. And its thinness would be easy to conceal and to leave the store with. But what to conceal it *in*? Her pockets could barely hold the snack packets. She passed the storefronts as she contemplated what style of bag would be easiest to steal but large enough to hold a knife—a backpack, a fanny pack, a satchel. She decided a backpack would be best, as it could also hide any other supplies, food, or drinks.

She passed an opened record store, its windows plastered with full-size posters advertising Chaka Khan's *I Feel for You* album and the soundtrack to *Breakin' 2: Electric Boogaloo*. Melissa thought wasting some time in there, pretending to be a shopper, would allow her to get her list of supplies finalized in her head. She opened the glass front door and was immediately met with the new-wave sound of Duran Duran's "Wild Boys" blasting over the in-store speakers.

"Mornin'!" the clerk yelled from behind the counter.

Melissa gave a half wave and kept her head down, her gaze on the carpet. She sped past the jazz section and into the rock area. If she thumbed through the records, appearing like she was a money-spending customer, maybe the clerk would leave her alone. She let multiple Pink Floyd albums lean toward her as she headed for the Prince records in the bin and got lost in admitting to herself that she couldn't just cold stab someone with a knife.

Even if the world would be better off without them, Mel knew she couldn't just slice or stab someone who would be fighting and flailing for their life. Mel acknowledged her lack of strength as a teenage girl—and possibly her lack of stomach to keep slicing and dicing until her victims were dead. *Vicki had been different*, she told herself. Vicki's death had been in self-defense, and Anya had been present—safety in numbers.

Mel got lost—not staring at but staring *through* the front cover art to Queen's *The Works* album—while ascertaining which method would be best for her to incapacitate her targets so she could then cut them with the least chance of resistance. She could strangle them first until they were unconscious, then stab them, but that would involve a sneak attack from behind and a possible struggle—and why not just keep pulling on the rope until they were dead?

She could hit them on the head with a blunt object—like Vicki—but that might involve several strikes to the head, and, at that point, Mel may as well just keep hitting them until they were dead, giving them ample chance to fight back. Nothing seemed clean or easy. She could—

"Can I help you find anything?"

Melissa jolted backward, dropping the album she had been holding.

"Noticed you had been staring at Freddie Mercury for quite a while. Thought maybe you needed some help making a decision."

Melissa blushed and eyed the Queen album lying on the floor now. "I ... I-I was just in my own little world for a minute."

The clerk bent to collect the record from the carpet. "If you like rock, you should really check out the new Bruce Springsteen album."

Melissa smirked at the clerk, who couldn't be any older than her. "Don't really like the full-out rock stuff. My favorite band is Wham!"

"*Ahh.* You like more of the new-wave, pop-rock stuff. Follow me." He moved a few bins down and turned to her, his wildly moussed hair not moving an iota. His icy-blue eyes seemed to pierce right through her. "Please tell me that you know these guys." He placed a record in her hand.

She locked gazes with him for a moment before she checked out his suggested band, unsure if he could see the heat that had risen to her cheeks. She chuckled and handed it back to him. "You're kidding, right? A Flock of Seagulls is already two years old."

The clerk smiled wide. "Yeah, maybe so. But quality music never dies. Those guys will be around forever. Their music is timeless. I've worn out two copies of that album already."

Melissa broke eye contact and looked at her sneakers, wishing to be away from him and wishing to never leave all at the same time.

"Name's Cash." He proffered his hand.

Melissa looked at him from the corner of her eye and snickered. "Your real name is Cash? C'mon."

The clerk's face reddened, and he stepped backward. "I … Well, I …"

"You just want to sound cool, so you gave yourself a nickname. I get it. Well, Cash, nice to meet you. I am Rainbow, but anyone who knows me calls me Melissa."

Cash nodded. "Point taken. Anyone who knows me calls me—"

"*Uh-uh*. I'm not ready to lose the illusion yet of Cash for"—Melissa swiped both hands in front of her and looked above his head, as if she were seeing his name in lights on opening night—"the super stud!"

They heard another customer enter the shop and glanced to the front door.

"What else you suggest, Cash?"

"I might quit while I'm ahead. I feel everything I've said to you so far has been ridiculed. How do you do that?"

"It's a talent. And, Cash, you certainly are not ahead."

"Excuse me!" the customer yelled across the store.

"I'll be right there!" Cash answered and focused on Melissa. "You're new here. I can tell."

"How so?" Melissa tucked a loose strand of hair behind her ear.

"You don't have that far-off, zombie-eye stare yet. Vegas will do that to someone."

"I'm here visiting my uncle. Got in yesterday."

"Oh, yeah? How long are you staying?" Cash leaned his elbow atop a row of records.

"I'm still waiting!" the customer yelled from the front of the store.

Cash shook his head and sighed. "Lemme go take care of this piece of sunshine. Don't go anywhere."

Melissa smirked and locked her gaze on him for longer than she had intended as he walked toward the impatient customer. Maybe she could use him to help her acquire some supplies—or maybe she was just so starved for friendship that didn't include a centuries-old witch and an army of ghouls.

She watched him hand a record to the customer and saw the customer's mouth say, *Thanks.* She turned back to the row of records, not wanting to make it obvious that she anticipated his return, not giving him the satisfaction of seeing her watch him. As she flipped through the vinyl, not really computing what she was looking at, she heard Duran Duran stop abruptly in the speakers, and, a moment later, she chortled when the already outdated—yet so-called timeless—sounds of A Flock of Seagulls filled the shop.

Cash appeared beside her.

"You just had to, didn't you? If I didn't know better, I'd think you were trying to run me out of your store with this." She pointed to the corner speaker without breaking eye contact.

"My mom doesn't let me play my music loud in the house, so the only time I can blast what I want to hear is when I'm working. I picked up some extra shifts during Christmas break just so I can have some relief from that hellhole of a house."

"What grade are you in?" Melissa felt herself relax just a smidgen.

"I'm a senior. Doing my best to blow off the rest of the year. I wanna be a rock star, and what respectable rock star has a college degree? Right?"

"Well, you're halfway there with that hairdo."

Cash tapped the top of his enormous bouffant. "You gotta look the part. How 'bout you?"

Melissa wrestled with telling the truth—recalling how much she hated it when Benji would call her Freshman or realizing she may never see Cash again and could add a few fictitious grades. Feeling the panic of time running out, her answer just slipped from her mouth without second-guessing it. "I'm still a freshman."

He nodded. "You gonna be around in a bit, Rainbow?"

Relieved he hadn't called her Freshman, she asked, "Why? You got some new Captain & Tennille you want me to hear?"

"Thought we could grab a cup of coffee. I get a break when the next employee shows up in, like, an hour."

Melissa thought an hour was just enough time to concoct a way to introduce the idea of him helping her obtain the supplies she needed to prove her worth to Anya. *Anya*—she hadn't even thought of the witch or the book or the Chosen One or the vultures or the cult since she had stepped into this store. Cash had proved a good distraction from the darkness and had made her feel like a giddy teenager again—normal.

"I'll come back to get you in an hour. It's a date," she said a little too cheerily for her liking and blushed. "I ... don't mean that we are ... dating now, or anything. I just meant ... that we—"

"You're adorable when you get flustered. Get outta here. I'll see ya in an hour, Rainbow."

She nodded once and stepped past him for the door. "You can call me Melissa, you know."

"Nope. As long as you're calling me Cash, then it's nicknames all day long."

She giggled. "Fair enough. Where can a gal like me kill an hour while waiting for a guy like you to be free?"

"Across the mall is a neat secondhand bookstore. They let you sit on these big comfy chairs and read anything you want without having to buy it first. It's run by an old lady who I don't think can see very well anymore."

"Sounds like the perfect quiet place while I'm waiting." Melissa gave him a thumbs-up and trotted through the store toward the door.

"No running in the store!" Cash called out playfully.

She stopped and turned. "Really? You yell something like that with *this* on the speakers"—she pointed up—"and don't expect me to make an 'I Ran So Far Away' joke?"

"I walked right into that one."

"I'll save you the embarrassment, Seagull Boy. I've ribbed on you enough today."

"I appreciate that, Rainbow."

Melissa turned to leave again but stopped and faced Cash one more time. "Oh, that hair is out of place." She giggled as she watched him delicately touch each stiffened strand to feel which one might be slightly askew.

"You're making me rethink coffee!" he yelled as the door closed behind her.

Melissa spotted the secondhand bookstore across the parking lot. It didn't seem to have a proper name—unless Used Books was its real name, as the generic sign over the awning implied. She entered, and already the glaring sunlight from the outside world vanished as the door closed behind her. All outside sounds also seemed to have been muffled instantaneously. In what little light did exist in the shop, she saw dust particles dancing to a ballet controlled by whatever breeze she had brought in with her. Musty shopworn smells hit her nose. Bookshelves covered every inch of the cramped room—floor to ceiling, wall to wall. Still, no one had greeted her.

She grazed her fingertips across the spines of hardbacks that looked to be a century old. She noticed no gaps existed in any of the displays, as if no one had actually bought anything from here. There also didn't seem to be any rhyme or reason to the order of the books. Melissa saw they weren't in any sort of alphabetical order—by title or by author—or even by chronological order of publication date. It felt like someone had just moved in, recently unpacked the moving boxes, crammed all their stuff onto the shelves, and decided to sort it out later.

And where was the storekeeper?

Melissa stopped to look at a book spine illuminated by a single strand of sunlight coming from over her shoulder. She had just read this novel last summer as part of her independent reading curriculum for entering high school, and scenes from it rushed through her head in warp speed. *Bingo!* The answer to her conundrum had been solved by this unlikely fifty-year-old novel. She grabbed the top lip of the spine and pulled *Why Didn't They Ask Evans?* by Agatha Christie from its spot. A plume of dust came with the falling-apart book.

Melissa leaned backward to peer to the rear of the shop. "Hello? Is anyone here?" She didn't get a reply. "If you can hear me, I'm just gonna sit here and read this book for a while." She waited again for an answer, but none came.

She sat in a red velvet-covered chair with a high back, like a throne, and gold-lined armrests. The chair felt and looked older than the book in her hands. She opened the front cover, and the cover fell diagonally sideways as the glue that held the spine to the pages peeled away from the book. Melissa supported the cover—now hanging on by just a thread at the top—from underneath with one hand and flipped through the musty and water-stained pages, looking for that one scene.

Old-fashioned typeset whizzed past her eyes as she hunted for the excerpt. A rustling sound came from what Melissa assumed was a back room, and she stopped flipping to stare at a door in the rear. "Hello?" she called out again, her voice seeming to die the moment it left her mouth, absorbed by all the books.

When she didn't get a response again, she resumed scouting for that scene. She knew she had found the correct chapter as soon as she recognized the setting. She stopped scanning and got lost in the chapter. And there it was, just as she had remembered—chloroform. It seemed so easy: douse a rag with the liquid, creep up behind the target, slap it across their mouth and nose, and render them unconscious.

Then she could do whatever she wanted to the body and take as long as she needed. That's how it worked, right? That's how it happened in this book and in the countless thriller movies she'd stayed up late to watch that her parents would have disapproved of. Seemed too easy but it was exactly what she was looking for—clean, low-risk, and foolproof.

She closed her eyes and fantasized about this being her MO; this would be what would define her as the killer. Her grandfather, the Wharf Killer, had studied under the Boulevard Killer, and now she would carry the torch and become the Chloroform Killer ... but maybe it was important to distinguish herself from all Anya's *male* killers who have preceded Mel. She needed something hip, something bodacious, something *modern* and chic.

Her eyes snapped open, and her heart raced—the Chloroform Girl! Menacing, empowering ... *Too much like a superhero name?* She'd have to ponder this choice a little more. Maybe it was too cheesy.

She sighed and dove back into reading. She would just read from this point on until it was time to meet Cash in an hour. Even though she knew the twist at the end, she still gobbled every word and devoured every movement the detectives made. The shop felt like it was getting hotter, and she tucked her legs underneath her to get more comfortable.

Thoughts of how to find chloroform started to plague her. Her attention waned from the words in the book and focused more on her uncertainty. *Did stores even sell chloroform anymore?* That could put a big dent in becoming Chloroform Girl. Could she make chloroform from regular cleaning supplies at a supermarket? Where would she even get that information if she could?

The shop door opened, startling her. She turned her head quickly, forgetting she had been alone inside someone's store this whole time; maybe it was the shopkeeper returning finally.

Cash entered instead. "There you are."

"What do you mean, there you are? You're the one who told me to come here, goofball."

"Well, I thought you had stood me up. My break started fifteen minutes ago."

Melissa slap-closed the book and jumped from the chair. "What are you talking about? I've only been in here for ..." She checked her watch. "Holy mackerel. I've been in here for almost an hour and a half."

"Time flies when you're having fun, huh?" He nodded to the book in her hands with his chin. "It's cool. I still have fifteen minutes left. I can drink a coffee in seven."

"Lead the way." Melissa slipped the book into its original slot on the shelf.

"Have a good day!" Cash yelled toward the counter.

Melissa turned. "Who are you—Wait a minute. No one's been here the whole time. Where did she come from?"

"You mean, like how you weren't here for ninety minutes without knowing it? I told you, I think she's blind."

The old woman behind the counter waved at them.

Melissa left the shop, shaking her head. She followed Cash across the parking lot to a café with outside seating.

"I got this, since it is a date and all." Cash smirked. "What do you drink?"

"I don't usually drink coffee, so surprise me."

He nodded and went inside while she sat at a table with two seats on the patio. When her back pockets hit the seat, she remembered the multiple packets of nuts she had hidden there. The bookstore's chair must have been too comfy for her to notice.

She mulled over her chloroform dilemma until Cash returned with two steaming cups of coffee. Before his bottom could hit his seat, she blurted out, "Do you know how to make chloroform?"

He paused in midair and stared at her. "Interesting initial topic on our first date. But I'll bite. Why?" His backside plopped the rest of the way into the chair.

Without rehearsal or choosing her words, she opened her mouth and let fly whatever wanted to come out. "Euthanasia. Back where I'm from, I live on a farm, and sometimes I help my dad put down the maimed animals." She couldn't believe how effortlessly the lie spewed from her brain, like someone else was writing her words for her and she was just the puppet. "I've been thinking of ways to make the"—she made a slicing motion across her throat with her index finger—"a little less painful or traumatic."

Cash nodded, seeming to accept this explanation as normal in her world. "Doesn't your dad, being a farmer, have access to medications or stuff that can do that? Why risk making an illegal and potentially harmful-to-*you* chemical?"

"I ... I-I ..." *Think, you idiot. Say anything.* "I want to surprise my dad, to show him I'm worthy of the family business. So I didn't want him knowing I was doing this. I want to stand on my own and carry my weight." *Phew.*

"I get it. Very admirable of you. I like it. You got spunk, Rainbow. Yeah, I can help you. I think chloroform is just bleach and rubbing alcohol. Mix it together, and the fumes could put anyone out."

She was surprised at how easy it sounded. She tried not to let her expression reveal her shock and excitement. She could fit a small bottle of rubbing alcohol and bleach, plus some rags and a large knife into a backpack. This was proving easier than she had anticipated.

"How's the coffee?" he asked, raising his chin.

"Oh, I totally forgot about it."

"I know. That's why I said something. Too busy thinking about chloroform. Having that come out of my mouth, I now think this is the weirdest date I've ever been on."

"I'm not scaring you off, am I?" She blew on her coffee to cool it down.

"I don't scare easily."

"True. I know your music taste."

"Let it go, Rainbow. Let it go."

She giggled and held her gaze with his. She felt her face warm and her knees tremble. "Do you wanna hang out after you get out of work?"

He leaned back in his seat and sighed heavily. "I can't today. Promised my mom I'd help her with some stuff she needs moved. What about tomorrow?"

Melissa swallowed her first sip of the coffee and went to answer, until she spotted Anya standing behind Cash.

"I'm delivering you to your uncle tomorrow, child. Don't go fucking up all our plans over this"—Anya looked down at his hair and scowled—"*boy*." She flicked a rogue strand of his hair, and Melissa almost burst into laughter.

"Tomorrow I have a full day with my uncle. Sightseeing, visiting, quality time—you know the drill."

Cash nodded. "Well, I'd like to see you again before you head home. Which, by the way, you haven't told me when that is or where that is—other than a ranch."

"Farm," she corrected him, which she found funny, since even *farm* was fictional. She eyed Anya for some answers.

"I don't know, child. How long *did* you plan to stay here? That one's on you," the witch replied.

"Christmas break. And I live in Montana." Melissa winced at the lie. She knew nothing about Montana. She wasn't even sure there *were* farms in Montana. She crossed her fingers that he wouldn't start talking about Montana.

"Okay then, Rainbow. You know where I work. I'll be there almost every day over break, always the morning shift. So I'll leave this in your court. If you wanna hang out more, hit me up at the store or call my house. If I don't hear from you, I'll know you hated the coffee." He laughed at himself and stood to go inside the café for a pen and something to write on. He returned with his number scrawled across a white napkin.

"Sounds like a good plan." She tucked the napkin in her front pocket. "I'll catch ya later, Cash."

He gave her a two-finger salute and headed toward the record store.

Anya swooped her long black robe around her waist and took his seat. "He's cute."

"Oh, stop it." Melissa crossed one leg over the other and took another sip of coffee.

"We've been here almost twenty-four hours, and the cult hasn't had any new additions."

Melissa glared at the witch. "It's been one night!"

"A night we can never get back."

Melissa leaned across the table. "I very highly doubt George or Grandpapa killed every single night."

Anya looked across the parking lot. "They killed every night they were available to. You were available last night. You just chose *not* to."

"You are impossible. I need a little bit of time to get the hang of this."

"You didn't need time in Stepp's office. Vicki's head didn't get bashed in by itself."

"It's like you want to rob me of any happiness."

"Is it happiness for the greater good knowing those bottom-feeders are out there, every night, soiling society?" Anya folded her arms, her pale face disappointed behind the black veil.

Melissa squinted and studied the witch from the corner of her eye. "I'm calling bullshit."

"I'm sorry? What was that, child?"

"I think I finally got you all figured out. All this righteousness of cleansing the Earth is bullshit. It's a facade for your real reasons to kill."

"Ha! This should be good. Please enlighten me, child, of what you think my motive is. I can't wait for this one."

"It's like the clouds just parted. You couldn't give two shits about any of us mortals. You're hiding behind that idea so you can build your army—your minions—for when you find the Chosen One and become immortal. For decades now, you've been lying to everyone just so you can grow your power and your numbers. We've all been taken for a ride, and I recently bought my own ticket."

"Are you done yet?"

"You are selfish and a liar and have not a shred of decency in you. I'm done, Anya. I'm clocking out. You can go have your stupid war with someone else. All those promises you've made me mean shit now. And here I was thinking I was doing something *good* for the world—for my community—by following your lead. You pathetic piece of—" Melissa grabbed at her throat as her air supply shut off.

Anya leaned her face forward so Melissa could see her through the black veil. "I have crushed cockroaches more important than you. Watch your tongue."

Melissa's eyes darted around as she saw red spots invading her vision from lack of oxygen.

Anya remained calm in her seat, her hands proper and ladylike in her lap, as she watched her apprentice squirm for a breath she couldn't take until Anya allowed her to. "Are you done?"

Melissa heard a high-pitched buzz in her ears as consciousness slipped from her.

"Oh my god! I think that girl is choking!"

Melissa heard the words way in the distance, spoken from another patron. Then two chairs squeaked backward as two people rushed to her. She felt hands on her body as someone stood behind her and pulled hard into her sternum. "Must be lodged in there good," Mel heard the man say.

She felt another sharp jab of the man's thumb and knuckles under her sternum. She focused on the witch, who remained sitting as stoic as always, grinning at Melissa. Mel pleaded with her eyes for the witch to release whatever spell was on her.

Anya flashed her three rows of fangs as a warning before releasing the spell.

Melissa gasped, heaved, and gulped in a bucketful of air. Her arms flailed, and she launched herself out of the chair.

The couple who had been trying to save her stumbled backward, surprised by the sudden movement from the teenager who had just been choking a second ago.

Melissa glared at the witch, who remained content and calm in her seat. In a flurry of anger, Melissa focused on the small table and pushed it with her gaze. The table launched into the air, flipping end over end like a car in an action movie, and sent her coffee spraying the couple who had been trying to save her.

The woman gasped, covering her mouth with her hand, and stared wide-eyed at the table as it crashed to the ground. "No one touched that table!" she screamed as she tugged the man she was with. "Did you see that?"

Patrons and employees from inside the cafe came outside to see what the ruckus was.

"I will *not* be your puppet, Anya!" Melissa screamed—at what appeared to be an empty chair.

The witch grinned and folded her arms.

"The girl is looney," the man whispered and ushered the woman to a car.

"Are you okay?" an employee asked, stepping closer to Melissa, while two other employees righted the overturned table.

"She'll be just fine," Anya answered the employee, even though she knew no one could hear her.

Melissa balled her fists.

"That was impressive." Anya spied the table being turned right-side up. "I didn't think you had that in you yet." The witch stood and smoothed out her robe. "Start making me some bantlings, and I can help you harness that power so you can move whole buildings." Anya slowly walked around Melissa but stopped right next to her ear. "You know that's what you really want, deep down."

Melissa closed her eyes and concentrated on her breathing, hating with every ounce of her being that Anya was right. Melissa only tolerated what she had to endure because she wanted a taste of that power. And she knew Anya wasn't full of empty promises, because she had seen the extent of Anya's power—something she wanted more than her own dignity.

When she opened her eyes, the witch was gone, and people were still staring at her, keeping their distance. The table was back on its legs, and the garbage she had jettisoned from it had been discarded in the trashcan. She hung her head and turned from the café, the backs of her eyes still tingling from the power that had exploded from them to make the table flip.

She knew she had to get herself back on course after tasting that little bit of power and knowing oh-so-much more was promised to her. She hadn't felt that alive … ever.

Melissa felt more confident this time, reaching for the long kitchen knife in Sears. She had swiped a gnarly backpack from a Jordan Marsh so easily that she thought they must have let her get away. Finding this mall was the best thing that had happened so far in her shoplifting spree; she had found a store for each item she needed. Glancing left and right to confirm the coast was clear, she hefted the backpack off her shoulder and slipped the kitchen knife inside. She headed for the exit, which spilled into the mall's long hallway.

A map of the mall's layout caught her attention, and she searched it for the next store she needed. She thought getting some industrial-strength rope would be a good idea, to bind her victims after the chloroform had taken hold; then she could carve them up, like a piece of meat. She found a hardware store at the far end of the mall and assumed she might find bleach and rubbing alcohol there as well, completing her shopping spree.

She trudged along the busy mall thoroughfare, passing an arcade already in full swing with buzzing lights and sirens and screams of joy from kids winning at pinball or Paperboy. She shook her head, pitying the mallrats whose biggest concern was getting to level five on Kung-Fu and choosing which fast-food place to eat at later. She smiled to herself, knowing she was on an important mission that benefited all of society. Maybe Chloroform Girl really *was* a superhero. Regardless of what she thought Anya's intentions truly were, Mel knew—in her heart of hearts—that *she*, Melissa, was doing this for the right reasons: to become as powerful a witch, a high priestess even, as Anya and really bring down the hammer on the slime that feeds off the streets.

She stopped in front of the hardware store and slid her backpack to her wrist; it was easier to slip items inside if it dangled by her thighs. She entered and noticed the clerk eye her suspiciously—what teenage girl would be shopping in a store designed for middle-aged men who were doing house renovations? She decided she would need to be stealthier and quicker in here than she had been in Sears, for she felt like she was under the microscope.

"Can I help you, miss?" the balding clerk asked.

Melissa couldn't help but notice a little venom in his tone. "My ... My dad sent me in with a list of items to get for him."

"Oh?" The clerk's eyes brightened, and his face relaxed. "I'm sure I could help with that," he said in a warm and relieved tone.

"It's fine, sir. I come to these stores all the time with my dad to help with repairs around the house, so I know my way around. I'm sure I can get along just fine."

"Oh, nonsense. I don't have any other customers to attend to. I'd be happy to help."

Melissa took a deep breath and threw caution to the wind. "Fine. I need a sturdy rope, some bleach, and a bottle of rubbing alcohol."

The clerk squinted at her, and she felt each second elongate as she waited for his response.

"*Huh*, well, if it's for your dad, I'm sure he knows what he's doing."

Melissa felt her heartbeat quickly decelerate. "Yes, sir. He's a supersmart man. I'm hoping to learn a lot from him." *Why do I sound like I'm Dorothy from* Wizard of Oz *right now? Stop it, Mel.*

"Always warms my heart when I see a young girl take an interest in home improvement. Or any young'in, for that matter. Do you know what gauge rope he needs?"

"A thick one. It's for holding … cattle." *Cattle? Really?*

"I think this one will do the trick." He placed a heavy bundle of rope in her hands. "And we keep all the solvents and cleaners in the rear of the store. Follow me."

Melissa hung the bundle of rope on one shoulder as she nervously followed the clerk.

"Here ya go, miss." He grabbed a jug of bleach and a bottle of rubbing alcohol but didn't hand them to her. "I'll bring them up to the counter for you. Was there anything else on the list, or was it just these?"

"Just these. Thank you, sir."

He nodded and traipsed to the checkout with the two chemicals.

Melissa's brain computed all possible options faster than she could decide on one that felt the best. Her hands shook as they neared the checkout. What to do? She couldn't pay for any of this stuff.

The clerk set the two containers on the counter and punched in some numbers to the register.

Letting her instincts take over, Melissa grabbed the two bottles, tucked the rope under an armpit, and bolted for the door.

"Hey!" the clerk yelled and ran around the counter to chase her. "Shoplifter! Stop that girl!" he screamed into the mall hallway as Melissa made a beeline for the nearest exit.

She glimpsed back at him and saw him dart into his store. *Probably to call mall security or the police*, she thought. She spotted an Exit sign at the mouth of a side corridor and took the turn. Doors were in front of her, and she never slowed as she barreled through them into the sunlight.

She strode across the parking lot—not too fast, as not to draw attention to herself—and didn't stop until she felt she had created enough distance from the mall. She meandered into a small park and sat on a concrete bench. With her heart still racing and her adrenaline surging, she struggled with shaky hands to unzip the backpack and cram in the two bottles and rope.

She groaned, let her head fall backward onto the top of the bench, and closed her eyes.

"Looks like you're preparing for a war party," a man next to her said.

Melissa flung open her eyelids as her heart hammered in ears. "You ..." she growled.

Baron crossed one leg over the other and intertwined his fingers so his palms rested on one knee. "Still trying to win Anya's love and affection, huh?"

"Get bent, asshole."

"I'm not the enemy, Melissa. I want you to see how she has manipulated every single person she has ever employed."

"I don't *work* for her."

Baron sighed. "That's not what I meant."

"I was hoping she had taken care of you," Melissa mumbled.

"Come again?"

"Yesterday Anya said she would take care of you. Obviously, she didn't."

"How do you know I didn't take care of her first?"

"Yeah, right." Melissa rolled her eyes. "I think you're jealous."

Baron snorted. "Jealous of what?"

"That she has her own army, that she's on the path to full immortality, that—"

"She only uses her powers for selfish and evil reasons?"

"You're the evil one. You keep getting in her way."

"I guess *evil* is just a matter of perspective, huh? Have you ever wondered why she just doesn't kill everyone herself? Why she always needs someone to do her dirty work for her? Don't you think it would be easier if she cut out the middleman and built her cult herself?"

"I ... Well, it's because ..." Melissa scrunched her face.

"See? There's no good reason. Not one I can think of."

"Maybe she knows something we don't."

"Maybe she's just a bitch who gets off on dragging people through the mire with her. She has destroyed everyone who has ever helped her. There's no escape from her tyranny."

"Why do you care so much what she does? Aren't you some powerful wizard or something yourself?"

"Something like that. And I care because I've been implored with keeping mortals safe from vultures like her."

"No pun intended, right?" Melissa chortled. "Why did you track me down anyway?"

Baron turned his body so he faced Melissa. "I'm here with Bridgett Hapney, and we—"

"Where is she?" Melissa stood, scanning the park. "She didn't get the message to stay the fuck away from me?"

"Calm down, firecracker. I was certain this would be your reaction to her, so I told her to wait at the hotel."

Melissa sat again.

"As I was saying, we came in the hopes to get you to believe a few things."

"Like …?"

"For starters, Anya has been hunting this so-called Chosen One for centuries. A lot of innocent people have died—*kids* have died. She'll never find the Chosen One unless they reveal themselves to her. There isn't someone who has a magic beacon of light shining from the top of their head, advertising they're the Chosen One. Anya's like a dog chasing its tail. How many more *innocent* people have to die? And I'm sure you don't want to be an accomplice to more murder, right?"

Melissa bit the inside of her lip and remembered Vicki.

"Anya trying to justify her actions as being a do-gooder is a farce. It's a fantasy she has told herself so many times over the centuries that she has started to believe it as truth, and now she can't see what is fabricated and what is reality. How many more people, like George Covington, like your grandfather, like *you*, will she drag down with her before she gives it up?"

"She only needs to be right once about the Chosen One for it to work and for it to all be over."

"Then tell me how many more Rose Covingtons need to be burned alive before Anya reaches that one she's looking for? It's been *hundreds* of years, Melissa."

Melissa scratched her head and felt her backpack get heavier in her lap with its murderous contents.

"I can tell you're wrestling with both sides of the coin. This is why I didn't let Bridgett come with me right now and why I left her in the hotel. But, if you wish, we can all sit down together and figure out an exit strategy for you. Madam Hapney didn't take what you did to her desk personally and wants nothing but the best for you."

Melissa let the nervousness of having to make her first kill-in-the-wild weigh on her shoulders, and she exhaled loudly through her nose. She looked Baron in the face. "It wasn't supposed to be like this. I can't stop seeing Vicki's beaten skull in my head. It was supposed to be an easy kill. Then me and Anya would be a team to do right. Now I'm hiding out on the other side of the country. I tried to kill my grandpapa, and I'm trying to get the knot in my stomach to go away so I can help add to the Mushroom Cult."

"See? Now you are coming to your—"

"So, if you would kindly fucking get out of my way"—Melissa rose and tried to tower over Baron—"so me and the high priestess can finish what we started, you piece of shit. You're like a black fucking cloud hanging over us, and you— *you*—are the one who's complicating this." Melissa balled her fists and clenched her teeth. "Now I understand why Anya despises you. Sometimes innocent people have to die for the greater good."

Baron rose, his chest bumping Melissa's nose as he grew taller. "That's just the brainwashed version of you talking. I can see a glimmer of the real you inside. Why do you keep putting up the wall when you start to show your true feelings on everything that's happening? What kind of hold does she have on you?"

Melissa growled, "She's given me a purpose, something I've never felt before."

Baron nodded in understanding—in more ways than one. "Don't do anything you'll regret or that you can never take back, okay? Be smart." He gestured with his head toward her backpack.

"If you are so all-mighty and powerful, why don't you just step in and stop me before I do, huh?" She touched her index finger sternly to his chest.

"You are so naive in how all this works. Madam Hapney and I will be watching closely. Try to keep your witch in check."

Melissa chuckled. "Tell that bitch I said hello."

"I'll tell her that you said you were sorry for what you did to her shop."

Melissa opened her mouth to retort, but Baron had vanished. She groaned and stomped a foot on the concrete pathway.

12: MAGICAL BAND OF FOOLS

Stepp sat comfortably on Anya's throne in the netherworld, playing with the voodoo doll in the witch's likeness. The bantling didn't know how long he'd been sitting here, waiting for his creator to return, but he knew time didn't pass the same here as it did out there. He also felt himself growing stronger with each passing second—minute, hour, week, month? He couldn't tell.

He hadn't quite gotten speech down yet—and, as far as he had seen, no Mushroom Cult ghoul had yet either—but he could control his limbs with resistance now instead of feeling like they were Jell-O, constantly flopping around. And that meant he had options.

He tapped a foot while he waited for the witch's return. He'd been waiting patiently since the tornado of vultures had removed him from the throne room and had dumped him on the outskirts of the netherworld, forcing him to clamber back here. *Stupid birds.*

He heard shuffling enter the throne room; it definitely wasn't Anya, but any slaughter would do at this point. Everyone needed to pay for his untimely death and being reanimated in this depleted form. He stood from the throne and tossed the voodoo doll to the floor.

Pum'kin stopped in her tracks, and her eyes widened.

Stepp descended the throne and shook his head. Oh, if only he could speak. He opened his mouth to try again to spew some witty and sarcastic remark he had been so revered for in life, but all that escaped was a chirp and a gurgle sound. He pursed his lips in frustration.

Pum'kin turned for the entryway, an unsettled look on her face, and Stepp lumbered as fast as his ghoul legs could carry him until he caught up to her. He used his bodyweight and momentum to knock her to the ground, then landed on top of her.

Pum'kin flailed hopelessly as Stepp sank his teeth into her cheek and easily ripped away a section of rotted flesh. She screamed from somewhere deep inside her chest as he spit the chunk onto the floor.

Stepp straddled her, letting her flail and whoop, hoping it would signal Anya that something was wrong so she would come to rescue one of her girls. Then he'd have Anya where he wanted her.

Pum'kin kept scratching for her missing cheek, almost squirming free in the process, so Stepp caught her flailing hands and pressed his knees onto each hand to keep them grounded. Her bark-scream grew louder but no sign of the witch still. Her wails of pain grated on his ears, like a jackhammer, and he wasn't sure how much more he could endure. If the witch didn't show herself soon, he'd have to do something to end the noise.

His gaze darted from entryway to entryway but no sign of Anya.

Pum'kin was finding her voice now, and her guttural squawks were turning into true screams.

A movement caught his eye from the opposite entryway. He smiled, knowing Anya would come sooner or later; she would never allow one of her lieutenants to suffer. The figure in the entryway stepped into the light of the throne room, and Stepp's devilish grin lowered into a concerned frown.

Ten of Anya's cultists shambled into the room, all with murderous intent written in their eyes.

Stepp sighed internally and understood Anya had sent her best soldiers to neutralize him instead of coming herself; this was proof that the message of pain from Pum'kin had been received loud and clear.

The gaggle of ghouls stepped forward in unison, and Stepp quickly buried his face in Pum'kin's neck and ripped out her throat with his teeth.

She bucked and arced her back as every muscle tensed, then she went limp and motionless, her gaze fixed on the approaching brood.

The ghouls chirped and whinnied at their fallen sister, then set their sights on the traitor.

Stepp rose, Pum'kin's blood staining his chin, and walked over her lifeless body toward the ghouls. He growled the best he could and curled his index finger, daring them to come closer.

Cyana charged first, both arms raised in a similar pose that Stepp had seen displayed by the dancing zombies in

Michael Jackson's "Thriller" video on MTV a few weeks ago for the first time.

Stepp held his ground, and when Cyana got within reach, he effortlessly grabbed the sides of her decaying head and twisted … until there was a *pop*, and her body crumpled to the floor. Stepp tossed her head at the shuffling ghouls.

Candy was in front and reflexively caught Cyana's head, like a bachelorette catching a bouquet of flowers at a wedding. She chirped and flapped her arms, sending the decapitated head sailing against a wall.

The rest of the cultists pogoed in place, terrified and unsure what to do next.

Candy waved for them to flee.

The gaggle turned and headed for the entryway from which they had arrived.

Stepp shook his head at their backs as they moved away from the throne room and strode toward the ghouls in the rear. He grabbed one girl's shoulder and spun her to face him.

Fear and desperation crossed Nikki's face.

He tilted his head and smirked before he ripped Nikki's weak arm right from its socket, grabbed her fingers with his hand, and used the stump to bash in her soft skull. With each raise of Nikki's disembodied arm, Stepp felt himself gaining strength and emotion. Back and smash, back and smash—her head was now just a caved-in puddle of goo on the throne room floor. He cocked back Nikki's arm one last time and flung it at the final ghoul escaping through the entryway.

It bounced off her head and sent her stumbling forward. She lost her balance and skidded face-first across the floor.

Stepp chuckled inside and realized he had one last main ghoul he could eradicate before the rest of them escaped.

The downed ghoul peered behind her as she got to her feet. When she saw Stepp charging for her faster than any ghoul had ever moved before, she opened her mouth in a silent scream. Cinnamon tried to drag her zombified feet faster, but her decrepit muscles and joints wouldn't obey.

Stepp launched himself at Cinnamon's waist area, but when he collided with her to take her to the floor, the impact was too much for them. He felt his shoulder dislocate, and when they landed, his knee twisted all the way around. He grunted in both pain and anger over his rotting body; no matter how strong he got in here, his body would always be a decaying vessel.

Cinnamon's forehead took the brunt of the landing, and her left eyeball popped from her skull. It rolled a few feet ahead, leaving behind a grizzly trail of brownish fluid that once—in another lifetime—had been blood. She chirped and gurgled, straining to reach for the lost eyeball.

Stepp used his good arm to prop himself onto his good knee, interlaced his fingers so his hands became an organic sledgehammer, and brought down his fists with all the might his rotting muscles could muster. With each downward blow, Cinnamon's squawks and chirps got softer and softer, until she was silent.

When he was certain she was dead, he leaned back on his haunches and panted. He wiped his good arm across his forehead to clear off the spattered blood and noticed movement from the throne room behind him.

He turned, still panting heavily, and scowled at the single vulture perched on Anya's throne—the voodoo doll of her in its beak.

Fuck you! he screamed in his head, but all that came from his mouth was a high-pitched neighing sound.

The vulture flapped its wings once before it took flight over his head and through the entryway, leaving Stepp alone with the carnage of Anya's high-ranking lieutenants.

Now with the front ranks of her Mushroom Cult eliminated, he thought he knew of a way to escape the terrible fate she had bestowed upon him … and only one man could save him.

13: RAPIST EYES

Melissa knocked on Starr's door in the two-four-two rhythm and waited in the night's cool breeze.

The door creaked open, and Starr eyed her. "Are you here for a place to stay, or do you need something … more?"

"Was hoping for just one more night here. I'll be staying with my uncle tomorrow."

Starr nodded once and stepped aside to let Melissa enter.

"Hey, chickee," Laura said from the sleeping bag. "You're here early."

Melissa adjusted her backpack on her shoulder. "Was hoping to hang out one last time before I permanently stay with my uncle." She heard the toilet flush from behind the closed bathroom door and raised an eyebrow.

"Remember. This place is always open for anyone who needs a safe place," Starr said, sensing Melissa's inquiry.

A woman in her twenties exited the bathroom, grazed the recliner chair with her thigh, and stumbled, her unruly fiery-red hair resembling wisps of smoke as she fell.

Starr caught the woman and lowered her to the floor. "Maybe you should consider just staying in tonight."

The woman slurred a few syllables that Melissa wasn't sure were real words.

Laura snapped once to get Melissa's attention and mouthed, *Shitfaced!*

Melissa stifled a giggle and nodded in understanding.

"I gotta get me one more tonight," the woman barely squeaked out.

"I think you've already had enough to drink tonight." Starr rubbed the rogue strands of hair from the woman's cheek.

"I'm not talking about drinks." Spittle flew from her mouth as she tried to get her tongue to properly form the words. "I'm talking about another *job*. Mack is expecting money from three jobs tonight, or he'll beat my ass again. I's only got in two fucks so far."

Melissa swallowed hard, with this reminder that Starr's haven was really a hideout for whores. She kept her head down but watched Laura. Everything she needed to kill Laura was in her backpack, but maybe this drunk woman would be an easier first sacrifice, since she was already more than halfway to unconsciousness already. Anya didn't need to know the specifics surrounding the girl; she just wanted to build Anya's army. Anyone meeting the criteria would do.

"Get a new backpack?" Laura asked, noticing Melissa staring at her.

"Who … the fuck … are you?" the woman asked, finally realizing someone else was there. "Never seen you before."

"She's new," Starr answered for her.

"Just fucking great!" The woman brought down her fist, like a hammer pounding an invisible nail in the floor. "Just what we need. Just what *you* need!" She pointed her hand-hammer at Laura. "More competition. There's already too many girls and not enough Johns anymore. Those classy so-called *escorts* on the strip are stealing our *bus-i-ness.*"

"I'm not one of you," Melissa mumbled.

"Two thousand a night, some of *dem* bitches are collectin'!" the woman continued, not hearing Melissa's reply. "Man, I'm in the wrong business."

"Or just working on the wrong side of the street," Laura muttered and smiled at Melissa.

Mel smirked at Laura's snarkiness. She hated that she was beginning to like Laura.

"You should just sleep if off here and start again tomorrow," Starr suggested.

The woman rolled over to a sitting position, crossed her legs, and harrumphed like a toddler. She burped so hard that she retched and covered her mouth to prevent any vomit from escaping. "Okay, maybe I should call it a night."

"*Mmm-hmm.*" Starr nodded. "And you get right back out there tomorrow and make up what you lost tonight, and Mack will never know."

"That sounds like a good idea, but I don't want to stay here. I need to sleep at home so I'm there when my baby wakes up tomorrow."

Melissa's eyes widened, and her lips pursed. *A baby?* She felt anger turn her blood to ice.

"I'm gonna walk her home. You good being here, just the two of you?" Starr asked Laura.

Laura raised the wine cooler she was drinking in a mock toast. "Paradise for sloths!"

Starr winked at her, then helped the unsteady redhead out the door.

"Want one?" Laura asked, proffering a wine cooler to Melissa.

"Maybe later."

Laura nodded. "Got a new sack, huh?"

"What? Oh, yeah." She let the backpack slide to her hand. "Went to the mall today."

"Looks like you scored a bunch of new stuff. Looks bustin' at the seams."

Melissa sat at the foot of the sleeping bag next to Laura and set the backpack behind her back to partially obstruct it from view. "Just grabbed some clothes and some toiletries."

Laura reached under her pillow to retrieve a small deck of playing cards that Melissa had never seen before and dealt the cards between the two girls.

Melissa raised an eyebrow at the unfamiliar designs on the cards. "What are you doing?"

"Passing the time with a round of Uno."

Melissa scooped up the seven cards in front of her. "What is Uno?"

"You gotta be kidding me." Laura let her hands fall hard in her lap for affect. "You've never heard of Uno?"

Melissa shook her head.

"Alright, well, get ready to have your little world expanded," Laura said with a giggle. She explained the rules as they played a mock game. Laura asked to see Melissa's hand so she could explain each card and what the most effective next move would be. After the scrimmage round, Laura collected the cards, shuffled, and dealt them again. "Ready for the real thing this time?"

Melissa grinned. "Bring it."

"Getting cocky already. I like it." Laura fanned out her cards in her hand, then playfully slapped Melissa's knee. "Amateurs first."

"Hey!" Melissa smiled. "Be careful. I'm a fast learner, and I'll kick your Uno butt before you know what hit you."

"Let the slaughter begin." Laura threw down her first card. "Bam!"

Melissa laughed, her eyes twinkling and free, then the reality of why she was here descended on her like a dark blanket, enveloping her in its grim embrace. She hated herself for starting to like her target. She hated herself for having such a good time with someone so dirty. She hated herself for not knowing whose hooks were really stuck in and controlling her anymore.

As the pile between the two girls grew higher, the laughter and playful banter increased. Melissa found herself getting caught up in making plans with Laura to hang out during the daytime, to do *friend* things, like get their nails done, see a movie, people-watch at the mall … She had to suppress her excitement and refocus on the mission. Laura would be her first gift to the ranks of the Mushroom Cult; she had to stop playing Best Friends Forever with this slut and get her head back in the game—the game waiting inside her backpack.

Melissa shifted her weight and got to her feet. "I'll be right back. Gotta pee." She hefted her backpack over her shoulders.

"Scared I'm gonna steal your stuff?"

Melissa froze, realizing how suspicious it looked. It wasn't that she thought Laura would steal from her; she was concerned Laura might snoop through it. "Heh, yeah, you're right. Still not over being mugged."

Laura nodded once and returned to shuffling the Uno deck for another round.

Melissa slowly lowered her backpack onto the sleeping bag and headed for the bathroom. She entered, turned on the light, and placed both palms on the side of the sink while she studied her reflection in the mirror.

Anya's image slowly slid from behind her head in the mirror.

Melissa didn't turn around but spoke to the witch's reflection. "Just a little more time, please."

Anya lifted her black veil, fully revealing her pale face. "We lost a handful of girls tonight."

Melissa spun to make eye contact with the witch. "What do you mean?"

"Someone killed all my lieutenants in one swoop."

Melissa reached behind her to grip the edges of the sink. "Wha … What the hell? All of them?"

Anya nodded.

"And you couldn't see it happening? Or the vultures didn't try to stop it? I thought you were all-powerful!"

"Keep your voice down, child. You don't want the hussy to get suspicious." Anya floated to the edge of the tub and sat. "I was meditating on locating the Chosen One. When I'm …" She sighed. "When I'm in that state, I can't see what's going on. I haven't learned yet how to meditate and keep watch over my girls." Anya glanced at Melissa with anxiety, confessing one of her weaknesses.

"I was warned that you aren't as powerful as you claim to be."

Anya rose from the tub's edge. "By whom?"

"Baron hung out with me for a bit at the park. He said … He said …"

"He said, what, child?"

"He said some things that made sense," Melissa murmured.

"We just lost every single important cult member tonight, and you're doubting our quest?"

"Not *our* quest." Melissa looked from the floor to Anya. "Just yours."

The witch slowly pulled her veil over her face, her features disappearing behind the fabric. "We need bantlings more than ever now, child. More than ever. This is a dire situation. No more excuses. You start bringing me new blood, starting with your girlfriend out there."

The weight of losing so many important cult members struck Melissa. With a tear hanging in the corner of her eye, she asked, "Pum'kin?"

"Dead. They're all *dead*, you stupid girl. At least, any who mattered. The ones who were spared are all the pea-brained ones I don't give two shits about anyway. We lost the brains and the brawn. Normally, I would care what quality of sacrifice you bring me, but these are extreme times. Literally, any piece of shit will do. So you start holding up your end of the bargain and go back in that room and start building the ranks, or I will strip you of the little power I have already gifted you."

Melissa balled her fists. "I won't do it."

Anya stepped forward so her putrid breath hit Melissa's face as she spoke. "You *will*. Or I will cut you myself."

Melissa glanced at the closed door and thought about the backpack's contents, just inches from her first intended sacrifice.

"And what better opportunity to do it than now, while it's just the fucking two of you," Anya growled through clenched teeth.

Melissa turned from looking at the door to glare at the witch, but she found herself alone in the bathroom. She sighed and closed her eyes, trying to squash all the feelings she'd recently developed for the stranger in the next room. After she steeled herself, she opened her eyes to see a black bird of prey sitting inside the tub. "And why didn't any of you stop whoever was doing it?"

The vulture tilted its head, its black eyes darting back and forth.

"I thought you guys were on our side."

When a knock sounded on the door, Melissa startled.

Laura asked, "You okay in there?"

"Coming right out." She turned on the faucet to feign washing her hands, counted to thirty, then turned it off. She opened the door and saw Laura had flopped back onto the sleeping bag next to Mel's backpack.

Melissa silently lambasted herself for not being more assertive or concocting a good excuse why she should have taken her backpack into the bathroom with her. She could have doused one of the rags she had stolen into the homemade chloroform and burst from the bathroom like a hurricane, using the element of surprise to buy her an extra second or two. But now she had already so-called relieved herself, and the backpack sat within an arm's reach from Laura.

Mel sauntered to the newly dealt game of Uno waiting for her and sat cross-legged across from Laura. "How long do you think Starr will be gone?"

"You can go first since I whooped your ass so bad in the first game. And I don't know. She could be gone an hour or so, depending on how hard it is to get Lucy situated where she'll be safe to sleep it off. And to make sure the baby is okay."

"How old is her baby?"

Laura shrugged. "We *can* talk and play at the same time, you know."

"Sorry." Melissa threw down the first card to start the game. "Were you just going to hang out here all night?"

"Taking the night off for some me-time."

"And here I am, keeping you company."

"I like your company. I see a little bit of me in you, before I completely gave up on a normal life. I don't want to see you lose that, like I did." Laura tossed down her color match card.

Melissa's gaze panned from her seven cards in her hand to her stolen backpack next to her.

"She was raped."

Melissa was snapped from her concentration of picking the next card—or killing Laura with the contents of the backpack. "Huh?"

"Lucy. You asked about her baby. That baby is from a rape. She refused to abort it though, because she bragged how it had been taken care of on a paternal level."

Melissa chuckled and tossed down her next card. "What does that mean?"

Laura leaned forward and spoke in a deep, low voice that Melissa had never heard from her. "She cut out both his eyes, buried his body in the desert, and keeps what she calls his rapist eyes in a small pouch under her bed."

"Body hasn't been found yet?"

Laura threw her next card on the pile and leaned back. "Nope. But they did find a ton of old graves. All girls. Skeletons mostly. They think they were all from the forties or something. Tied them into a case that had gone cold back then. Some motel killer or something."

"The Boulevard Killer," Melissa said, staring hard into Laura's eyes.

Laura snapped and pointed at Melissa. "Yes! That's what they called him. You've heard of it?"

Melissa eyed her backpack again. "I went through a phase where I was interested in serial killers. I found the Boulevard Killer special, because my uncle was a reporter during all those murders, and he had reported on a lot of the girls' deaths. He still has a lot of the newspaper clippings, so I could ask him personally about that time and what it was like."

"Oh, man. Your coolness level just went sky-high in my book. Can we, like, be best friends or something?"

"Or something …" Melissa mumbled.

"So, you wanna show me what clothes you got at the mall today?" Laura leaned forward and grabbed the backpack's straps.

Melissa, like a deer in headlights, didn't move. She knew she should snatch the bag back and protect her identity, protect her future, protect her path to power. But she just sat there, crushed under the weight of the comfort Laura made her feel.

"This feels stuffed to the brim." Laura set the backpack between her legs and grabbed the zipper. "I hope you got some good deals. Marshalls is the boss for deals. Unless you lifted all this stuff ..." Laura stopped unzipping and smirked at Melissa. "I'm just kidding with ya."

Laura got the zipper up and around the top hump of the backpack, and Melissa closed her eyes. When she heard Laura yell, "What the fuck!" Mel sprung open her eyes and saw the backpack fly across the room, strike the wall, and fall to the floor, then the zipper slowly closed the opening.

Laura jumped to her feet and squinted at Melissa. "That's the second fucking time something has flown across the room, and both times have been when you were here. Who the *fuck* are you?" She took an aggressive step toward the teenager.

Melissa stepped backward and watched the backpack, lying on its side across the room, begin to levitate.

Anya held both straps but only by the tippity tops of her fingertips, like it was a piece of clothing covered in feces, and offered it back to Melissa. "I think you lost something."

Laura watched the backpack float across the room toward them and stop in front of Melissa. "What the fuck is going on? Are you a witch or something? A demon? How ... How are you making it do that?"

"Kill her now or I will," Anya said. After a moment of silence, she said, "Then at least take the motherfucking bag from me!"

Melissa reached out, took the bag from Anya's fingers, and eyed Laura.

"Does she want to see the truth? We can show her the truth," Anya said.

"I-I think you need to go," Laura said and gulped.

"She was my only fucking friend, you bitch!" Melissa yelled.

Anya fully materialized, growled with her three rows of fangs fully extended, and lunged for Laura.

Laura's eyes widened, and she backpedaled so quickly that she stumbled over the sleeping bag and fell on her back. She raised both hands in a defensive position to block whatever satanic creature was attacking her.

Anya stopped, stood upright, and tilted her head. "A better life awaits you, Laura. All you gotta do is take my hand and let Melissa show you the way." Anya extended her arm to the shaking girl on the floor. "You can be best friends forever. Just come with us." Anya turned her head to Melissa. "I can't believe I am doing your dirty work *for* you. God, you are so fucking weak, child!" She refocused on Laura. "Are these scaring you? I'll put them away." She retracted her rows of fangs and lifted her veil to reveal her pale face. "See? Not so bad. My name is Anya, and I'm looking for a few good girls, like you."

Laura's gaze darted to something behind Anya, and when Anya turned to look, she saw the front door closing—Melissa was gone.

The witch spun and took chase through the door. She flicked her finger in the air as she passed through the threshold, slamming the door behind her. She saw Melissa about a half block ahead, sprinting. Anya raised herself slightly off the concrete of the sidewalk, abandoning her mortal legs for the quickness of flight, and glided like a shark toward the fleeing teenager.

Behind her, she heard Laura banging on the closed door, screaming to be let out, but the spell Anya had placed on the door would hold her inside for a few more minutes.

Anya clotheslined Melissa across the shoulder blades from behind and took them both to the ground. "Where you goin', child?"

Melissa pushed herself up with her palms and stopped in the plank position. "I don't even know anymore." She let her body fall to the sidewalk and sobbed.

Anya lovingly tucked a strand of Melissa's hair behind her ear. "That was a pitiful display of power back there. Borderline weakness. Are you sure you're cut out for this life?"

Melissa tilted her head just enough where she could see the witch from the corner of her eye. "I … I just want to go home. I-I want my mom."

"I think you mucked that up when you killed the secretary. You're a killer now, whether you're comfortable with it or not." Anya lowered her face to Melissa's ear. "You bashed in her fucking brains. You made your Hell, now lie in it."

Melissa's sobbing increased to full-blown tears and hiccups.

"You disgust me. Now, you can either go back there and finish the job on that *whore*, or I can relieve you of your apprenticeship and call the vultures to rip off your fucking limbs, one by one. Your call, child." Anya exaggeratedly tapped each long fingernail into the concrete in an inpatient rhythm.

Melissa's forehead rested on the sidewalk in defeat. "Tomorrow. I'll do it tomorrow."

Anya rose to stand over the sprawled teenager. "I expect that hussy in there"—she pointed at the house behind them, where Laura's wails to be let out had grown to a feverish pitch—"to be among the Mushroom Cult ranks within twenty-four hours."

"If you need her so bad, why didn't you just do it when we were in there?" Melissa's voice was muffled from the crook of her elbow.

"I'm not the one who needs to work through their doubt and trepidation. How would you learn anything if I'm doing your work for you?" Anya released the binding spell, and Starr's front door flung open. "Meet me at the chess table tomorrow morning at ten o'clock so I can deliver you to your uncle."

Anya vanished just as Melissa saw Laura come barreling through the front door. She got to her feet, grabbed her backpack, and took off, like a starter pistol had been fired.

14: SCARLET FEVER

"You look worse for wear," Anya said, materializing behind Melissa in the tree line overlooking the empty chess tables.

Melissa did not turn around to greet the witch and remained silent.

"Your panties still in a bunch about last night?" Anya asked in a pouty tone. "C'mon. Let's get this over with so you can focus on your real responsibilities. Where does this so-called uncle of yours live now?"

Melissa continued staring forward. "I think he'd be at his restaurant. We should start there."

"Fair enough." Anya grabbed Melissa's dangling hand, and the landscape flashed purple.

Melissa startled and looked behind her to see Anya had transformed into a voluptuous thirtysomething woman with impeccable hair, resplendent eyes, and Barbie-like skin. Her yellow sundress flowed behind her, matching her bright and glamorous makeup. Melissa shifted and felt the gravel from the blacktop of Steel's Taco Shed's parking lot under her sneakers.

"Ready?" Anya asked, her voice singsong and as sweet as honey.

"You do know Uncle Hank is a queer cowboy, right? You won't woo him with that getup."

"Just follow my lead and try to hide any expressions of surprise you might have." Anya sashayed forward toward the Taco Shed's front doors.

Melissa gulped, willed her racing heart to slow, and followed the witch-turned-debutante.

Anya entered the taco shop and stopped, putting her hands on her hips. "Hello?"

A worker stuck their head around the grill station. "We don't open for another hour, ma'am."

"I'm not here for the food. I need to see the owner. I have his niece with me."

Joel stepped from behind the kitchen and into the dining room. "I ... I didn't know Hank had any siblings."

"He's not my real uncle," Melissa said, her voice squeaking. "He's my grandpapa's best friend."

"*Ooh* ... you're from our new Massachusetts location. He talks about you guys quite often. He's at Castaway's, right next door, helping with some construction or something."

"Thank you. We'll go see him there." Anya winked at Joel, and he blushed.

Melissa and the witch left the Taco Shed and found Castaway's Eatery. Anya pulled open the door and entered as three men turned to look at them.

"Mel?" Hank stepped forward and stopped. "What ... What are you doing here? Is everything okay?"

"Mr. Steel, I presume?" Anya proffered a hand.

Hank reached to shake it but never took his gaze off Melissa.

"My name is Eva, and I found this young lady hitchhiking on the highway with nothing more than the clothes on her body and that backpack on her shoulders. I just knew I had to help her. She told me that she was headed to Vegas to see her favorite uncle Hank. Well, I just couldn't let this sweet child make the trip alone, with all the crazies out there nowadays."

"You hitchhiked?" Hank glared at her, then bent forward in a deep, wheezy cough. "Do your parents know you left?"

Melissa lowered her head. "I ran away. I didn't know where else to go. I thought you'd help me."

"But, good Lord, love! Massachusetts to Vegas is a long trip for a girl to take on her own. It's not like I'm around the corner." Hank finally regarded Anya. "And thank you, Eva. That was very kind of you. Seems Mel had a guardian angel looking out for her. Can I offer you any compensation for your inconvenience? Gas money or a taco salad on the house?"

Anya feigned a giggle and flapped her hand forward. "Oh, it's not necessary. Just glad I could get this precious one to you safely."

Hank turned a hard stare to Melissa. "You do know I have to call your parents, right?"

"Can't I just stay here for a bit?"

"What happened, Mel? It must have been something bad to make you come all the way here. You don't get frazzled very easily."

Melissa remained quiet and played with something on the floor with the toe of her sneaker.

"Is everything all right, Hank?" Floyd asked, joining the circle.

"This is Travis and Gwen's daughter. She came out to see me."

Floyd smiled. "Nice to meet you. Hank talks a lot about your whole family."

"Nice to meet you, sir—"

"I'm Eva. It's a pleasure, I'm sure." Anya extended her hand.

"Floyd Covington. Likewise, ma'am."

Melissa's heart burst in her chest as she glanced at Anya, who had taken a half step backward and seemed rattled.

The witch quickly composed herself and regained her stoic stance. "Floyd Covington. Any relation to George Covington?"

"He's my brother. Do you know him? You're too young to know him."

"My grandmother was friends with his wife and poor … poor Rose." Melissa saw Anya/Eva's eyes grow sinister. "That story of her burning like that, just tragic! That would have made her your niece. How absolutely terrible."

Floyd looked to the ground and furrowed his brows, visibly working through the emotions. He inhaled sharply through his nose and pointed his chin to Anya's forehead so he was looking over her, not making eye contact. "Yes. Tragic. One of the worst weekends of my life. I would rather not discuss it."

Anya smirked, pleased with the proverbial knife she had just twisted in another family member of the girl who had been so wrongly identified as the Chosen One. "Well, I guess

I should leave you to it, now that Mel has been delivered, safe and sound."

The third man, who had been standing with Hank and Floyd when they had entered, leaned into Floyd's space, and tapped his wristwatch. "I'm on a schedule."

"Right, right." He smiled at Melissa. "Sorry, but time's money. His time spends my money." He turned and followed the contractor to continue reviewing the layout for the new extension for the eatery.

"Thank you again, Eva," Hank said and looked down at Melissa. "Are you hungry, love? Floyd's granddaughter is out back and just made pancakes. She's about your age." Hank put his arm around Melissa to steer her into the back kitchen.

The double swinging kitchen doors flopped outward as Floyd's granddaughter stepped into the dining room. "Grandpa? Where do you keep the syrup?"

Melissa flinched when she felt what she thought was a bee stinging her elbow. She rubbed her arm and looked back to see Anya/Eva wide-eyed, staring at the girl across the room. Inside Melissa's head, she heard Anya's raspy growl. *She's the Chosen One! I've never been so sure in my life.*

"There should be a bottle in the smaller refrigerator. Not the big stainless-steel one!" Floyd called out from across the restaurant.

The girl turned and disappeared through the doors.

"You guys can hang out this morning," Hank said and led Melissa toward the kitchen. "Floyd's looking to extend the dining room, and I promised him that I'd help with the plans. He sometimes brings his granddaughter here to help seat customers."

Maybe I wasn't completely wrong about Rose, Anya continued talking to Melissa. *Maybe I had the right bloodline but the wrong generation.*

Melissa shook her head slightly so Anya could see her displeasure in her wrong calculation all those years ago.

Yes, she's the one. I can feel it, child. The Covington line will bring me immortality. I knew I was right. Rose was just a hiccup. If you want to get in my good graces again, give me Laura for the cult and get the Covington girl alone so we can finish what I started centuries ago ... and you'll finally get your carrot.

Melissa heard the front door open, then close, and knew Anya/Eva had made her exit. Eva's job was over; she had delivered Melissa to Hank, with a somewhat believable story. Now Melissa was tasked with two initiatives: kill Laura for the cult and make friends with this stranger's granddaughter so she can be slaughtered in sacrifice to make Anya immortal and to promote Melissa to Anya's current status. *What could go wrong?* she asked herself.

Hank whispered, "She's younger than you but could use a friend." He pushed through the double swinging doors, and Melissa saw Floyd Covington's granddaughter sitting at a small break table, with a television blaring in the corner above her head.

Melissa wanted to wait as long as possible before making eye contact with the girl who she was required to fool and to destroy, so she focused on Kermit the Frog on the television, already in the middle of singing "Rainbow Connection" on a banjo while sitting on a log in the swamp.

"Scarlet, I'd like you to meet Melissa. She's an old-family friend."

"Hiya!" Scarlet said through a mouthful of pancakes. "Hold on one sec." She grabbed the TV remote, lowered the volume, and swallowed the food. "Sorry. Have a soft spot in my heart for *The Muppet Movie*. Want anything to eat?"

Melissa's stomach gurgled at the sight of real food—something she had not eaten in two days. She tried not to seem overanxious, but she nodded quickly. "Thank you."

"Pancakes and syrup?" Scarlet asked, getting up to fix a plate.

"Yes, please."

"Have a seat."

Melissa slid into the other seat at the small table, shuffled the backpack off her shoulders, and glanced at an array of Muppets now singing and swaying in unison on the screen.

"I'm gonna go help Floyd with the contractor. You'll be okay here for a bit?" Hank asked.

Melissa nodded and waited for Hank to catch his breath again. "Uh-huh. Thank you, Uncle Hank."

"No problem, love." He gave her a quick peck on the top of her head and left the back area through the double swinging doors.

"You from around here?" Scarlet turned to put a sopping pile of pancakes in front of Melissa.

"Massachusetts. Salem."

"*Ooo*, like where all the witches live?" Scarlet slipped back into her chair.

"Not as glamorous as it sounds."

"Or as creepy?"

Melissa chuckled. "Or as creepy."

Scarlet shoveled in another forkful of breakfast. "High school?"

"Freshman."

Scarlet swallowed, and her eyes brightened. "Do tell! I'm in eighth grade, and I can't wait to go next year. I'm so excited. Is it a lot different? I'm just *so* over all the little boys, ya know? I hear high school is when there are men."

Melissa almost choked on her food. "I think you're getting high school mixed up with college. At least, at my high school, the *men* are just the same boys from middle school, except they now have bigger egos."

"*Ew.*" Scarlet sat back in her chair and let her body slump. "That sounds even worse than eighth grade."

Melissa chuckled. "It's what you make of it."

"Do you have a boyfriend?" Scarlet leaned in.

Melissa hadn't thought of Graham since before she had fled. "Kind of."

Scarlet smirked. "Is he a senior?"

Melissa hesitated for a moment—this middle-schooler was a stranger, after all—but something about her charisma made her feel innocent, safe. "He's already graduated college."

Scarlet slapped a hand over her mouth and leaned sideways to see if any grownups were around. "You're dating, like, an adult?" she whispered.

Scarlet's reaction made Melissa feel less like a little kid. She felt powerful, confident. "Yep. You'll see. The high school boys are not worth the gum on the bottom of your shoe."

"I have gum on my shoe?" Scarlet lifted a foot to inspect the sole of her Keds.

Melissa chortled. "I like you."

"*Aww.*" Scarlet put a hand on Melissa's wrist from across the table. "I like you too."

"You also don't have many friends, do you?" Melissa peered at the girl from the corner of her eye.

"How'd you guess?" There was a long pause. "It's because of my love for them, isn't it?" She pointed her chin toward the television.

Melissa almost spit her mouthful of food across the table. "I think it might run deeper than your Muppet fandom." She took a moment to scrutinize the girl's clean but messy hair, tidy but clashing-colored outfit, and pimple-free but also makeup-free face. "You're cute. I think you'll do just fine in high school. You'll just need to find *your* peeps, ya know what I mean?"

Scarlet nodded. "Nobody at my school likes the things I do. I'm hoping high school will change that."

Melissa twirled her fork between her fingers. "I always thought middle school was like eating at a food truck, and high school is like a mall food court—lots to pick from."

Scarlet laughed so hard she snorted. "I like that. Well, I can't wait to get out of line at the food truck and walk around the food court!"

"That's the spirit."

"Wow, you just must be so cool and popular at school."

Melissa felt herself blush. "So, what's there to do around here for kids our age?" She noticed Scarlet swooned when she compared them as equals. "I mean, I don't know anyone here, and I'm only here visiting for a few days, until my parents come get me, so if you wanted to hang out, like, tomorrow afternoon, what could we do?"

"You wanna hang out with me?" Scarlet pressed an open palm against her chest.

"Yeah. Do you have any special places you like to go to? Any secret caves or anything like that?"

Scarlet snickered. "This isn't Salem!"

Melissa scrunched her face in confusion. "You think Salem has a lot of caves?"

"Well, duh. Where would all the witches live if there weren't so many caves there?"

Melissa slowly nodded and raised an eyebrow. "*Riiiiiggggghhhht.* And the moon is made of cheese."

"I know!" Scarlet slapped the table. "It's that crazy? I almost didn't believe it when I first heard it."

Melissa swallowed hard. How could she lead the human equivalent to a lost puppy to her demise? "Well, you, Scarlet, are just adorable. Let's have a picnic."

"A picnic! Yes! There's a spot in the desert where I sometimes go to when I want to write poetry on the weekends. Do you write?"

"*Nah*, I save that stuff to the people with actual talent. Like you."

"Oh, quit it. Anyway, I go out there with my headphones and just get lost in my poems. I like it because it's away from people but not too far out that I need a car."

Melissa had to consciously stifle an evil grin. "Headphones. We haven't talked about music yet. My favorite band is Wham! Your turn."

"Oh, I don't listen to bands. Only composers."

"Ah, okay. So, Madonna? Olivia Newton-John? Prince?"

"Who?"

Melissa shook her head and smirked. "You know, 'Let's Get Physical'? Maybe you should prepare yourself so high school won't be that different than middle school."

Scarlet tucked her legs underneath her in the chair. "I'm such a square."

"Okay, well, so what songwriters *do* you listen to? Are we talking old-fart music?"

"I said composer, not songwriter. Schubert. Tchaikovsky. Wagner."

Melissa dropped her forehead onto the table, making a loud *thunk*. "You gotta be kidding me." She raised her head slightly to look Scarlet in the face. "This is what we're going to do. Tomorrow we'll pack a lunch and go to your spot, and I'll show you a whole world in music that you might need to survive next year."

"Deal!" Scarlet clapped. "And I'll return the favor and play you Beethoven's 'Für Elise.'"

"Which is …?"

"The greatest piece of music ever composed in the history of … well, ever!"

"Can't wait," Melissa grumbled.

The double swinging doors flung inward, and Hank and Floyd entered the back area.

"Alright, Mel. I'm all done here. Come on. We'll head back to the house so we can call your parents."

"It was nice to meet you, Melissa," Floyd said. "I hope you two got along splendidly."

"Oh, Melissa is, like, my new best friend. We're going to have a picnic tomorrow and listen to music. She's totally boss." Scarlet turned her focus from her grandfather to Melissa. "So, wanna just meet here tomorrow at noon? We can walk there."

"Perfect."

"The desert … how fitting and ironic," Anya said, standing next to Scarlet.

"I'm ready to go, Uncle Hank." Melissa grabbed her backpack, refusing to acknowledge the witch's presence, and gave a half wave to Floyd.

Hank and Melissa maneuvered through the dining room, out the front door, and toward Hank's car in the lot. Once both were situated and Hank had pulled from the spot, he asked, "So, do you want to tell me what's really going on?"

Melissa watched the landscape pass by the window faster as the car accelerated onto the state route. She bit a fingernail, formulating what and how much she should say.

"If something bad happened or someone did something inappropriate to you, you came to the right place. But I wish you hadn't made that trek across country yourself. You can tell me anything, love. No matter what it is."

Melissa didn't stop watching out the window when she asked, "Do you promise not to tell my parents if I tell you?"

"Cross my heart and hope to be straight."

Melissa took a deep breath and released it slowly through her nose. "I got mad at someone and set their desk on fire."

"At school?" he asked in an almost yell, then gulped for a full breath of air as his lungs constricted.

"You promised."

Hank sighed. "You're right. Go on."

"No. It was at a shop. A psychic's shop downtown. I ... I didn't like the things she was saying, so I set her desk on fire and almost burned down the shop."

"So, are you running from the fuzz or your parents?"

Melissa finally unglued her gaze from the passing houses to look at Hank. "Both. The cops came to the house to question me about it, and I freaked out and took off."

"Arson is a big deal, love. But you're young and have never been in trouble before. Sometimes we have to sit up and take our medicine."

"I know. But I also swiped my dad's gun and then got it stolen during the trip here."

"Oh, Mel, Mel, Mel ... This just keeps getting worse. Is there anything else?"

Other than bludgeoning an innocent woman to death in her office, trying to kill my grandpapa/your best friend, and now planning to kill a hooker, plus sacrifice an eighth grader to some higher power, so my witch friend, who controls an army of dead prostitutes, can become immortal? "Nope, nothing else."

"Alright, you got spooked and ran. We can get through this. Do you want to talk to them, or do you want me to?"

"Could you please?" She batted her eyelashes at him.

"Sure thing, love. How's school?"

"Fine."

"How's your grandfather?"

Melissa cringed. "Last I saw him, he seemed ... fine."

"Good, good."

They drove in silence for a few minutes, then Hank turned on the radio by the knob, and a song that sounded like it was playing from an archaic turntable came through the speakers.

Melissa concentrated hard, trying to place the melody. "This is the song at the end of the movie *The Shining*."

Hank took his gaze from the road for a moment to glance at her. "Don't know that movie."

"Stephen King. Horror stuff."

"Your dad lets you watch horror movies?"

Melissa chuckled. "Who says he knows?"

"And this is why you're on the run. Mel, you are a great kid. Please don't go down a path you won't come back from."

"I won't."

Hank harrumphed. "Famous last words."

Melissa fingered the strap of her backpack lying in her lap and closed her eyes, dreading the inevitable phone call home. She must have dozed off, because the car jerking over the bump, heading into Hank's driveway, startled her eyes open.

Hank parked, and Melissa followed him into his house.

"You can sleep in the spare bedroom. You remember where that is, love?"

"Uncle Hank! It hasn't been *that long* since we've visited."

He nodded and headed for the kitchen phone.

She found the guestroom, tossed her backpack on the bed, and crept into the living room to eavesdrop on his conversation to her parents.

"Yeah, she seems perfectly fine. No injuries. A nice woman drove her some of the way. Looked out for her. … Okay, yeah. … She can stay with me until you get out here. … Just let me know when you get a flight. … He is? When did that happen? … Heart attack? … Oh, well, that's good. Send him my love. … Okay, hold on. Melissa!"

She entered the kitchen with her head down.

Hank held out the phone and coughed into the crook of his elbow. "Your mother wants to talk to you."

She shuffled forward and reluctantly accepted it. "Hi, Mom." She grimaced when the ear-piercing sound of her mother's voice echoed through the phone in a half-relieved/half-livid tone.

"What were you *thinking*, Mel? You had us scared to death!"

"I know, Mom. I'm sorry."

"I don't know whether to ground you or to kiss you when I get there. Across country? Really, Mel? And your dad is so angry that he's refusing to come to the phone. But he's relieved you're not dead or kidnapped."

"Yes, ma'am."

"We're gonna try to fly out there tomorrow. I'm just happy you're safe with Hank. I'll want to know everything, *everything*, Mel, when we get back home. No secrets. The only way your father and I can help you is if you tell us everything. Truthfully."

"Yes, ma'am," she mumbled.

"Let me talk to Hank again please. And, Mel? I love you."

"Love you guys too." Melissa handed the phone to Hank and headed for the guestroom. She closed the door and turned to see Anya standing in the corner, veil pulled down.

"I've left you a present. Check your backpack."

Melissa spied the bag on the bed and noticed it seemed bulkier. She unzipped it and removed the maroon-colored, leather-bound book with the metal triangle and single eye.

"You'll need to brush up on your lines for tomorrow. Remember, we get one chance. If you flub the words, we can't start over. It's a one-shot deal."

"I remember." Melissa lightly caressed the cover with her fingertips. "I hope you're right this time."

Anya stepped closer to the center of the room. "I have never been so right about this. I have never felt such a draw, such a yearning, from someone before. I know it's her. I even *saw* the halo above her head. She's the Chosen One—the one I've been looking for—waiting to be born. The Covington heritage is stronger than any of them realize."

Melissa flipped through the pages until her gaze landed on the familiar passage she was required to read aloud when Anya killed the Chosen One, to raise the witch to divinity.

"Practice those lines again and again. They need to come from your mouth as fluid as saying your own name."

Melissa looked up from the book at the witch. "And then I can be you?"

Anya flicked her black robe behind her. "As soon as I am fully transformed, I will bestow what you deserve."

"I don't exactly like the way you said that."

Anya cackled. "Come, child. You know I wouldn't recant my promise."

"And what happens with Scarlet? Does she become part of the cult?"

Anya pressed her palms together, as if in prayer. "Sadly, the sacrifice is a complete one. Scarlet hasn't done anything to stain the Earth, so she will go peacefully to Heaven, leaving me with her essence and ascending me to divine priestess." Anya separated her hands and lowered her gaze at Melissa. "But you still need to rebuild my ranks." She stepped closer. "You will slaughter that whore tonight and start earning your keep around here!" She took another step closer. "You must prove to me that you are worth my title and status. If you can't kill one measly little street-rat, then you are *nothing* to me." Anya spit on the floor at Melissa's feet. "Building the army is your *only* purpose right now."

Melissa glanced at the opened backpack.

"Your tools are all in there. All you have left is to test yourself, up here." Anya tapped her temple with her index finger.

"My parents are probably flying in tomorrow to take me home."

"They won't get here before lunchtime, right? Even if they catch the first plane out, we'll be done with Scarlet in the desert by the time they get here, so them coming will be moot. The sacrifice will be done, and you'll have taken my throne in the netherworld, all before they can even land at the airport. So no need to stress about *their* plans. We only need to focus on ours. If ours go correctly, none of what they do will matter."

Melissa realized the witch made a good point. Why worry about her parents coming to get her if she will be the Mushroom Cult High Priestess before they can even land? And the first step to get that title was to make Laura a part of the cult.

SALEM, MASSACHUSETTS; 1984

15: STRUCK BY LIGHTNING

"Hey, Dad," Travis said as he surveyed Smith from the hospital bedside.

Smith squeezed his son's hand and coughed. "Any news?"

"She thumbed a ride to Hank's."

Smith squinted. "In Vegas?"

"Yeah," Gwen said, coming to stand beside Travis. "Hank called us. She's safe, but we'll fly out in the morning to get her."

Smith nodded. "Tell Hank I said hi and that I'll come visit him when I'm out of all this." He motioned to the few wires still connected to his body.

"You're looking better, Dad."

"Doctor thinks I might go home day after tomorrow, as long as everything remains status quo. What about the young'ins?"

"Addie and Shaun are staying at your place with Mom."

"*Ahh*. Wynn must be over the moon right now, having her two tykes staying with her and me out of the house." Smith chuckled, and it turned into a coughing fit. "Gotta get that under control, or they won't let me leave."

"You'll get there," Gwen said. "If you need us for anything, just call us at Hank's. We'll probably get a hotel room for tomorrow night and fly home the following day."

"You don't want to stay and make a Vegas vacation out of it? God knows, Hank'll feed you three times a day from the shop."

Travis smiled, trying to lighten the mood. "He might have the best tacos I've ever tasted, but even this taco-lovin' guy would get sick of them after a while."

"Did you tell Wynn it was okay if she brought the kids by to see me? I think I'm feeling well enough now. Don't want to scare them none though, seeing me like this."

"I told her that it was her call, and we'd be fine either way," Gwen said.

"I think Mom's actual words were, 'It would take getting struck by lightning to keep me from seeing my man.'"

Smith laughed, and, this time, his chest did not tighten enough for him to feel the need to cough. "Well, that's reassuring. No chest spasm."

"See, Dad? You're on the mend. We love you, and I'll make sure to bring Mel by when we get back."

"Yeah, it'll be the only place she's allowed to go, except for school, until she's twenty-one," Gwen added.

"You never gave me any problems, Travis. We were blessed to have you as a son. I guess all my dirty deeds skipped a generation."

"*Thanks*, Dad. You could've kept those dirty deeds to yourself."

"*Argh*, get out of here, you lovebirds. Go get some sleep and go get my granddaughter!"

Travis and Gwen kissed his forehead and turned to leave the hospital room.

"And tell that nincompoop Steel that he still owes me bigtime for that Roxanne business!" Smith yelled after them as the door closed, leaving him alone with the beeping monitors and the sound of the city outside the window.

LAS VEGAS, NEVADA; 1984

16: ANARCHISTS OF GOOD TASTE

Melissa closed her eyes, held her breath, and turned the doorknob to Hank's bedroom to be as quiet as possible. She let the door creep open just enough to confirm that he was asleep—eyes closed, mouth opened, snoring loudly. She inched the door closed until she knew the latch was in the doorjamb and slowly released the knob.

She spun in the hallway, hefted her backpack more securely onto her shoulder, and padded through the house and out the front door into the moonlight. She tried to get her bearings on how to get to Starr's neighborhood, but she realized she would have to go the long way, to not get lost. She figured if she could get to the Taco Shed, then, from there, she knew the way to the park with the chess tables. After that, she knew the way to the strip and Starr's street.

Mel just needed to ensure she wasn't mugged again. She realized how much easier this would be if she still had her dad's gun and not a backpack full of chemicals and a knife—and how easier it would be if she genuinely didn't like Laura so much. In a different place and time, she knew they could be fast friends.

But this wasn't the time nor the place for friendships.

She found the Taco Shed, using signs to downtown, then located the park from memory. She passed the park, headed toward the strip, and reviewed the kill scene in her head, repeating the steps so it might just be muscle memory when she was there in person.

She played out the actions of her coming behind Laura with the chloroform rag—that was how the movies portrayed it being most effective—and lowering her to the ground, then wasting no time by stabbing the girl as many times as she could in the chest and stomach. Hopefully, it would all be over quickly and with little resistance.

The nightlife sounds of the strip increased, as she knew she was getting closer. She rehearsed the steps of the kill again in her head as she jogged across the strip and into the shadows of Starr's street. She ran through all the scenarios of what to do if Starr was there with Laura—how to get Laura out of the house, alone—or if even multiple people were there too.

Mel knew this had to be quick, leaving no opportunity to get sucked into chitchat or an explanation of what had happened last night when Anya had appeared and when Mel had taken off from the house. She knew it had to be wham, bam, thank you, ma'am.

She crouched against a tree and watched the house. She couldn't tell how many people were inside or if Laura was even in there. She saw a figure pass by the side window, so at least one person was there. A different-size figure then stopped in front of the window, and Melissa could tell by the silhouette of the wild hair that Lucy was back. Mel couldn't tell if that first figure had been Laura or Starr or a stranger.

The back door opened, and Melissa ducked down farther, almost resting her forehead to her knees. She watched from the corner of her eye as two girls she had never seen before exited and lit up cigarettes. The loud voices from their palaver bounced off the exteriors of the neighboring houses.

Melissa wondered how long chloroform lasted in a rag before it lost its potency and would need to be doused again. She had been afraid to prematurely soak the rag for that reason—also because she didn't want to knock herself out while waiting. She took a deep breath and contemplated soaking the rag now and waiting here outside the house, either for everyone to leave or for Laura to be on her way, hopefully alone.

The two unknown girls snuffed out their butts and returned inside. The rear screen door slammed shut as their voices became muffled again in the house.

Melissa unzipped the backpack and left it open. She figured it would be easier to get to the ingredients if she needed them fast.

A car approached slowly, and she watched it with her chin down but her eyes up, hoping it would roll by and not pull into the driveway she sat next to under the tree.

As she sighed in relief when she watched it pass, she heard the front door of Starr's bungalow open and close. She watched Laura bounce down the few front steps and head away from Melissa, alone.

Melissa felt her throat tighten in panic, fear, and anticipation. Completely disregarding stealth, she dumped the backpack's contents onto the ground and grabbed the rag.

She tossed it over one shoulder like a bar towel and fumbled with the caps to the bleach and rubbing alcohol. She set the bleach on the ground—but on a protruding tree root—and the bottle toppled. The liquid made a *gah-lub, gah-lub* sound as it emptied onto the grass. She panicked and right-sided the bottle, the fumes from the spilled bleach burning her nostrils and blurring her vision.

She glanced down the sidewalk and saw Laura getting farther away. Mel lay the rag on the ground and poured the remainder of the bleach bottle's contents onto it. She thought she could actually taste her esophagus burning. She gagged and coughed, then unscrewed the rubbing alcohol bottle and turned it upside down so all its contents landed on the bleach-soaked rag.

She coughed air deep from within her lungs and felt like she couldn't take a strong-enough inhale to replace what she was losing. She prayed she wouldn't succumb to the effects of the makeshift chloroform before she got the rag around Laura's nose and mouth.

Melissa stood, tucked the knife into her back pocket, slung the backpack over her shoulder—which now only contained the rope—and disregarded the two bottles under the tree as she bolted in Laura's direction. She felt her heartbeat in her ears, and her breath felt like it was on fire when it hit her top lip while she ran, rag in hand, held low with an open palm, as if she were approaching the opposite team to give them a low-five after a soccer game.

She wished with all her might that Laura would not hear her coming and wouldn't turn around. That was how it mostly happened in the movies.

She hunched as she ran, trying to control her breathing and to not have a cough explosion. She scanned the road and the opposite sidewalk. They were alone. She no longer feared the chloroform not working, since she had used the full bottles to soak one rag, but now fear of failing rose to the surface—failing the actual kill of driving the knife into Laura's organs.

No time to think anymore, as Laura's backside was now in striking distance.

Melissa raised her rag-holding hand like a catapult in front of Laura's face and pulled toward her when she felt the rag connect with Laura's face. Melissa tugged Laura's body against hers, applying further pressure onto the rag.

Laura flailed and reached behind Melissa's head to grab a fistful of hair. She pivoted her face to distance her nose from the rag and elbowed Melissa in the gut while yanking her hair at the same time.

Melissa stumbled backward, the rag falling to the sidewalk. She didn't know whether to nurse the section of hair that had almost been ripped out or to put pressure on the section of her stomach that felt like it had been shot. She doubled over and looked up at Laura.

Laura stood, facing her, panting, her gaze darting between Melissa and the crumpled rag on the sidewalk. She slowly bent to retrieve the cloth, never removing her gaze from Melissa's face. She brought the rag to her nose and flinched. "Really, princess?" Without warning, she raised her leg and dropped her foot onto Melissa's thigh like a sledgehammer.

Melissa grimaced and cried out, clutching her leg.

"You honestly thought all it takes is slapping a rag over someone's face, and they just pass out?"

Melissa raised one hand as she saw Laura cock back an arm and let a fist fly into her mouth. She thought her jawbone had exploded in her cheek.

"You watch too many movies. And you're too gullible."

Melissa stumbled backward and tried to get into a fighting stance. Her body trembled all over, both from adrenaline and fear.

Laura removed a shiny object from her back pocket, made a few magician-like movements in the air, and a blade seemingly appeared from nowhere. She pointed the tip at Melissa. "Survival of the fittest, bitch!"

Melissa closed her eyes and pulled her elbows into her gut to protect her vital organs. She felt the blade puncture the soft tissue just above her waist and then pull out. She wailed in pain and fell to her knees. She saw blood covering her left elbow.

Laura stepped backward to assess the damage and tilted her head. "You're even too chickenshit to run. Worthless. I told you the streets would eat you alive. Why'd you make me do it?"

Through tear-stained eyes, Melissa saw Anya appear behind Laura, and relief washed over her. "Oh, thank God," she mumbled. She didn't know how she'd repay the witch, but she knew she'd be indebted to her for a very long time, for Anya coming to her rescue—yet again.

Melissa's eyes widened, and her mouth fell open when she saw Anya just fold her arms, like someone bored waiting in line. Then the witch grinned.

Laura's boot collided with Melissa's temple, and the girl half-spun onto the sidewalk.

She stayed in a crawling position on her hands and knees. Blood soaked the side of her shirt, and every inch she moved sent painful waves cascading through her muscles and bones. She glanced over her shoulder to see Laura approaching again, the butterfly knife extended, and Anya keeping perfect pace behind the whore, as if Anya were attached by a rope to Laura, who was towing her forward.

"Help me!" Melissa screamed to Anya.

"We're beyond helping. I'm gonna fuck you up!" Laura answered, assuming the plea was for her.

Anya raised her index finger and ticked it back and forth, like a pendulum. "You reap what you sow, child."

"You betrayed me!" Spittle flew from Melissa's mouth as she glared at the witch.

"*I* betrayed you?" Laura said. "You just tried to kill me. And, out here, the punishment for attempted murder is death."

Anya gave a cute little wave to Melissa, as if she were acknowledging an infant in a baby carriage.

Melissa turned her head and crawled up the sidewalk toward Starr's house. Maybe if she could get someone's attention … "Anybody! Help me!"

Laura stomped on Melissa's ankle to halt her crawling advances and drove the butterfly knife into the girl's calf.

Melissa reached back and screamed. Blood now soaked her pant leg, and the pain was excruciating, whether she moved her upper body or her legs. She collapsed to the concrete, her cheek and nose grinding into the small pebbles. She closed her eyes and waited for certain death. She knew trying to return to a normal life was futile—not after Vicki's murder and her attempted murder on her grandfather. Maybe it was better to jump off the cliff and try again in the next life.

Melissa kept her eyes closed, but no final blow came. She opened the eye not pressed into the sidewalk and looked behind her.

Anya was picking at her nails, looking overly bored.

Laura had discarded the knife and was holding the rope from Melissa's backpack. "We're a single unit out here on streets. A single organism. What happens to one, happens to all."

Melissa swallowed hard and tried to ask what she meant, but the pain coursing through her body was too great for her to formulate cohesive words.

Laura unraveled the rope and wound it around Melissa's ankles.

"Need help with that?" Anya asked, leaning toward Laura. "*Nah?* Okay. It's all you." The witch winked at Melissa. "I love it when they can't hear me. But I'm superstoked to have a front-row seat for whatever she plans to do to you." Anya glided so fast next to Melissa's ear that the girl didn't even see the witch move. Then she growled, "Because you deserve every horrific thing she has planned for you, you fucking failure and disappointment."

Melissa tried not to choke on the witch's pungent breath.

Laura flipped Melissa like a pancake and bound her wrists together with the rope.

Melissa squirmed, like a fish out of water, but the searing pain in both halves of her body made it a haphazard attempt at escape.

Laura grabbed the chloroform rag, pinched Melissa's nose closed until her mouth gasped open, and shoved it into her mouth.

Wrung-out drops of bleach and rubbing alcohol dripped to the back of her throat as she flailed and bellowed a muffle cry.

"I just love what you've done with the place!" Anya said to Laura, standing over Melissa's face. "I'd say it needs a full remodel. How about we bash in her brains? Or … I have a better idea. One that will hurt her even more."

Laura wrapped the end of the rope around her palms, dug her heels into the sidewalk, and pulled Melissa toward Starr's house.

With malicious intent, Melissa darted her gaze between Laura and the witch, who only she could see and hear. As the back of Mel's head bounced over the cracks in the pavement and her limbs screamed in agony, she rolled her tongue behind the chloroform rag and pushed as hard as she could to expel the gag from her mouth. The fumes made her feel light and floaty, but now she understood the error of her ways—trusting what she had believed in movies to translate to real-life reactions.

Her shirt had now rolled to her shoulder blades, and she could feel road rash along her back as Laura pulled. Mel finally collected enough air in her lungs to muster a scream and opened her mouth, but her lips were slammed shut. She frantically looked at the witch, who was following the procession just beyond her feet, walking at the same pace Laura was dragging her. Melissa tried to peel open her lips, but they felt stitched together.

Anya grinned. "This. Is. So. Much. *Fun!*"

Melissa strained her eyes over her forehead to see where Laura was dragging her and noticed they were headed for the same tree she had been hiding underneath.

When Laura reached the base of the tree, she unraveled the rope from Melissa's ankles, took the slack, and heaved it over a low-hanging branch. She pulled, and Melissa lifted into the air, just by her wrists. Laura pulled again, and now Melissa's feet dangled a few inches from the ground.

Melissa felt her knife wound in her side stretch open as her torso dangled, her weight held only by her wrists.

"I'm going to gut you, you pig," Laura said.

Melissa flopped back and forth, trying to gain purchase on a tree root, to alleviate the pressure in her side. She strained to glance down and saw blood flowing faster from the stretched-open wound than she thought was normal. She took a breath to calm and to center herself, then squinted at the rope, directing all her energy to burn through it. But she didn't feel the familiar tingle behind her eyes, when her telekinesis would gather power for release. It felt … *normal.*

Anya clapped and jumped up and down. "I can giveth, and I can taketh away. You, you runt, are as powerless as you were the day before I graced you with my presence."

Melissa directed her spiteful gaze at the witch in front of her, then saw what remained of the Mushroom Cult behind Anya, moving as if choreographed in those old-time musicals. Melissa's eyes widened as she realized she was either going to die at the hand of her intended victim or at the hands of the army of ghouls she had been so desperately trying to lead.

Black feathers filled the night sky as vultures landed on telephone wires and branches around the kill site. They hissed and flapped in place.

Anya reached into her robe and slowly, tauntingly, removed the Mushroom Cult book. "I'm taking it back. You'll have no use for it, for where you're going."

Melissa had almost forgotten about Laura while concentrating on the ghouls, the vultures, and the book being back in Anya's possession, until she felt a jab into her side. She looked left and saw Laura winding up for another punch.

"I can't believe you tried to kill me. If I could kill you and bring you back to kill you again, I would." She let another fist fly, and the blow had Melissa's mouthful of air unable to release, with her lips seared together.

Mel swung gently from the tree, feeling like her shoulders would rip from their sockets. She almost wished that would happen; it might lessen the pain from the wound in her side being stretched by gravity and force.

She noticed Laura had disappeared behind the tree and tried to catch a glimpse of her. Was the death blow now coming? Was this the end? She made eye contact with Anya, pleading for any help, then tried to fold her body in half from the new pain.

Laura had gathered a palm full of sand and smooshed it with all her might into Mel's knife wound.

Melissa screamed from behind her spell-stitched lips in short, rasping bursts and bucked her body, the rope now cutting through the first layer of skin on her wrists. Every move—every *thought*—now brought more ripping and tearing to her body. She eyed Anya one last time, hoping for a shred of mercy from her mentor.

Anya sighed, raised the veil from her pale face, and pursed her lips. "Fine. It's too cliché to let this tramp kill you." She turned to the brood behind her. "Girls?"

The Mushroom Cult materialized from their cloak of invisibility and, to Laura's perception, appeared from thin air in front of her.

Both her arms went limp as she stepped backward and stumbled over a tree root. She landed on her back and quickly scurried on her hands and feet.

The ghouls marched forward, their eyes trained on their target.

"What the fuck are those?" Laura yelled.

Melissa noticed a light turn on in Starr's house. She knew if Laura wasn't silenced soon, they would have more to deal with than just the whore backpedaling right now.

Anya twitched a finger, and Laura's elbows and knees snapped in the joints' opposite direction.

Her back hit the ground, as bones protruded through her skin in all four spots. She opened her mouth to scream, but what remained of Anya's army had swarmed her.

Melissa choked down some rising bile when she heard the munching and chomping and gnashing of the cults' teeth into Laura's flesh and muscle. Mel noticed the vultures studying the frenzy, waiting for their turn to claim and to liberate the living dead—adding one more number to the ranks.

Starr's front door swung open, and Anya twitched a finger again. The door slammed in Starr's face. A muffled "What the fuck?" came from inside the house as they heard Starr rattling the doorknob, trying to open it.

The space between Melissa dangling on the tree and where the ghouls were devouring Laura filled with the flapping of black feathers. Melissa could no longer see what was happening through the wall of birds. She noticed a figure approaching, and Anya emerged from the monsoon of black.

Anya stopped and stared silently at Melissa.

Melissa grunted through her skin-stitched lips, every tendon burning in pain, every ticking second closer to passing out—hoping death comes quickly.

The storm of vultures behind her lifted skyward, and Laura's body was gone. Melissa knew Laura had been escorted by the birds of prey to be reanimated and gifted back to Anya. The remainder of the Mushroom Cult fell into ranks behind the witch, all facing Melissa.

"Destroy her," the witch growled to her brood. "And there'll be no salvation by the vultures for this one. Consume her, down to every last ligament and vein."

Melissa's eyes widened, and she bucked as she realized she would not find death through hanging and bleeding out, but through the razor-sharp teeth of a swarm of ghouls slowly consuming her.

Anya vanished, and the girls shuffled forward, mouths opened, already drooling.

Melissa closed her eyes, grimaced, and turned her head to the side in anticipation of the feeding. She took a deep breath and held it—anything that might lessen the inevitable pain. Her wounds and dislocated shoulder caused her to exhale sharply, so she forced herself to take another breath and hold it. What was taking them so long? Any second now, they would descend upon her flesh.

A strong arm cradled underneath her knees, and another scooped her body under her shoulder blades and started walking, carrying her like a new bride over the threshold.

She felt her release from the rope and opened her eyes to see the sidewalk was empty of the walking dead. Now untied, she pointed to her lips and screamed from her throat to bring attention to the flesh-stitches. Her mouth opened, with no residual pain or tearing, as the stitches released and disappeared, and every ache and wound melted back to feeling normal. "I never thought I'd be this happy to see you again!" She wrapped her arms around his neck.

Baron shushed her. "Gotta get you back to the hotel. Hang tight."

Instead of seeing purple when Anya would teleport her, Melissa saw a flash of orange behind her eyes and the feeling of all her molecules being pulled. The orange faded, and she was still cuddled in Baron's arms but in a hotel room.

Hapney stood from a chair and trotted toward them. "Is she okay?"

"She is now." Baron set Melissa on her feet. "Still feel any pain?"

Melissa rubbed each wrist where the rope had been supporting her and felt no burning anymore. She looked at her side and saw her wound was gone. "I feel fantastic!" She swallowed hard and stared at her sneakers.

"Are you okay?" Hapney asked.

"I said, I was fine."

"I don't mean physically. I mean"—Hapney touched the top of Melissa's head—"up here."

Melissa trembled and couldn't stop the flood of tears. She grabbed Hapney and pulled her close, crying in her blouse. "I-I'm so, so sorry," she said between choking on tears. "I was so scared. I thought I would die. And I'm so sorry I tried to hurt you."

Hapney rubbed Melissa's head and squeezed her. "It's not your fault. That witch had her hooks in you. She's very influential." Hapney held Melissa an arm's length away but kept her hands on the girl's forearms. "She needs to be stopped.

We need you to be strong one more time so we can end this once and for all."

"She left me for dead!" Melissa wiped a droplet of snot from the tip of her nose.

"She leaves everyone in a wake of death," Baron said, sitting on the bed. "I've spent the last few centuries trying to reverse the pain she brings on those who don't deserve it."

"Anya creates suffering, and Baron is the healer," Hapney said. "You're lucky he was out looking for you."

Melissa eyed the warlock. "Why couldn't you save Rose from burning to death? She didn't deserve to die."

"I'm not all-seeing. I can't be everywhere at once. I didn't even hear about Rose until the next morning. I'm not a god. I only found you tonight because I was looking for you. Rose was never on my radar."

"Can Anya hear us right now?" Melissa asked.

"I have a soundproof shroud over the room," Baron answered.

Melissa went to the window and surveyed the street below, the flashing Hotel Esper sign splashing hues of sea-green onto the sidewalk and the tops of the heads of the passersby. "She thinks this girl, Scarlet, is the Chosen One." She spun to face Baron and Hapney. "She wants me to get close to her, to hang out with her, so Anya can make the sacrifice."

Baron shook his head. "Who is Scarlet?"

"The granddaughter of the Castaways Eatery's owner, the business next to the Taco Shed. We tentatively made plans for tomorrow. She wants to bring me to the desert to listen to music and have a picnic."

"I bet Anya thought that was the perfect spot," Hapney said.

"And she probably just loves the irony too," Baron said, rolling his eyes.

"She took my book, and I don't have any powers anymore." Melissa guiltily eyed Hapney.

"We just need to lure her out there, and I will finally put an end to this mess," Baron said.

"You'll kill her?" Melissa asked. "Why have you waited this long to do it? Why didn't you kill her after the Rose incident? What makes *right now* different?"

"Only the Chosen One can kill her. It's written in all the books of spells. Each book contains the same verbiage. Anya knows I can't kill her. She knows only the Chosen One can. That doesn't stop me from telling her to her face that I should have killed her, but, if I do, then I break the code, and I'd lose all my powers too. This is why she's so hellbent on finding the Chosen One and killing her; in addition to the sacrifice awarding her divinity, they are Anya's only kryptonite."

"I'm surprised you know what that is," Hapney said with a sly smile.

Baron chuckled. "I'm a few hundred years old, not a hermit."

"So, Scarlet has to kill Anya?" Melissa asked. "I don't think that kid could fight her way out of a paper bag."

"She's ..." Baron took a deep breath. "She's not the Chosen One."

Melissa raised her eyebrows.

"That's another reason why we have to stop her before Scarlet becomes another Rose."

"Then who *is*?" Melissa asked.

Baron glanced at Hapney but remained silent.

"Oh, c'mon! Don't tell me you don't know."

"We know who it is," Baron answered without breaking his gaze at Hapney.

"Well, are you gonna tell me? If I'm going to help you, I need to know who—" Melissa clasped a hand over her mouth. "It's *you*! You're the Chosen One?"

"I've gone to great lengths to keep Bridgett's identity from Anya," Baron said. "All the while training her to one day be powerful so she can stand a chance against the priestess."

"Baron recognized what I was when I was a little girl. He's been in my life since then, grooming me, training me, preparing me for what I'm destined to do."

"Rid the fucking world of that witch," Melissa finished. "But I thought the Chosen One had to be a virgin."

Hapney nodded silently.

"*Ohh ...*"

"I told you Baron got to me early. Once I realized how important I was to the greater good, I have followed my teachings and training to a *T*—which included staying pure for the fight."

"You guys should totally hook up when this is all over," Melissa said with a chuckle and thought she saw Hapney blush. "I can't believe I set the Chosen One's desk on fire," she mumbled.

"My biggest concern," Baron said, "now that Anya doesn't have a curator anymore—Stepp is a ghoul, your grandfather has so-called retired, and she has abandoned you—is she'll go rogue and be even more unpredictable. This is why I feel it's paramount we bring the fight to her as soon as possible—as in, tomorrow in the desert."

"Anya already knows you've made these plans, right?" Hapney asked. "Stick with the plans. We'll be watching from the other side and will strike when she shows herself to claim Scarlet."

"Won't she be suspicious about how I'm not dead? Not to mention that I'm fully healed? That would tip *me* off that something seemed fishy and that it was a setup. She knows Baron is the only one powerful enough to put this masterpiece back together." Melissa giggled as she twirled and ran her hands down her sides, like Vanna White, revealing a new word puzzle on *Wheel of Fortune*. "I mean, I was inches from my body ripping itself apart."

Hapney snapped her fingers and pointed at Baron. "I've got it. We don't give Anya time to question it, but we force her to appear."

"Go on …" Baron nodded, his eyes glistening.

"Melissa, you go on the picnic, like normal. When you get out there and confirm you're secluded from anyone seeing you, pounce on Scarlet and tie her up."

"Wait. What?"

"Hang with me for a sec. Tie her up, and, yes, Scarlet will be terrified, but you need to play the villain role at this point."

"Oh, I'm pretty good at that. Just ask my siblings."

"After you have Scarlet tied up, scream for Anya to show herself, or you'll kill Scarlet."

Melissa smirked. "I get it. Because Anya will show purely from fear of me killing who she believes in the Chosen One."

"Exactly. The moment she appears, Baron and I will take over and do what should have been done long ago."

"So, we're using Anya's panic of losing the Chosen One to draw her out, not giving her a chance to question why I'm healed and there. You guys will need to be quick. She's not stupid."

"No, she's not. But she's desperate and greedy," Baron said. "This might just work."

"Afterward, we'll have a lot of explaining to do for poor Scarlet," Hapney said.

"She's not the brightest bulb on the Christmas tree. I'm not worried about that. If she tries to tell this story to anyone, they'll probably roll their eyes and chalk it up to her weirdness."

"Alright, so it's a plan," Hapney said.

"Just don't leave me hanging out there," Melissa said. "Anya will kill me as soon as she shows up."

Hapney took the girl's hands in her own. "I promise we won't let anything happen to you. And I forgive you. I know that wasn't the real you back at my shop."

Melissa nodded, trying not to cry. "Thank you," she mustered in a cracked whisper.

"Now we gotta get you back to Hank's. We can't have him waking up and seeing you gone," Baron said. "Tomorrow, wake up like normal, go about your morning, and meet Scarlet as planned."

Before Melissa could reply, orange flashed behind her eyes, and she found herself standing in Hank's guest bedroom.

SALEM, MASSACHUSETTS; 1984

17: DIE A HUMBLE DEATH

Stepp, now with renewed control over his fine motor skills, paced the hospital room in front of Smith's bed. The ticking clock and beeping from the machines were the only sounds. A typical Salem winter sky of overcast clouds blocked out the moonlight and left the hue from the hallway lights seeping through the bottom of the door as the only means to see.

Stepp glanced at his decaying hands and noticed the goo stains from killing Anya's girls. As he paced, he realized he had a decision to make. The drive was strong in him to keep returning to the netherworld to pick off Anya's army one by one until none were left, but the drive to just sever his own cord so he could literally rest in peace was a tad stronger.

The heart monitor kept time with Smith's heartbeat as Stepp contemplated what his final move would be.

Beep. Beep.

He stopped pacing and approached the bedside. He watched the hospital blanket rise and fall with Smith's breathing. It wasn't labored anymore, and Smith seemed to be regaining strength. Stepp knew Smith would be discharged soon, and, if that happened, Stepp would have lost his chance at making it look natural.

Beep. Beep.

Stepp quickly swiped away a string of drool that had escaped his rotting lips, then crossed his arms. He watched Smith's eyelids twitch in his sleep and wondered what the old man was dreaming about. He moved to the other side of the bed and peered down at the Wharf Killer. No, he refused to be this man's bantling. He refused to be under the witch's thumb for the rest of eternity.

The door opened, and the reach of the hallway lights brightened the room.

Stepp stood motionless as the nurse entered to check Smith's vitals and readouts. She grazed Stepp's tattered and bloodied clothes as she passed to sign off on the clipboard hanging over Smith's head on the wall. Stepp inhaled deeply as she passed again, reveling in her scent of flowery perfume. So young. So fresh. So … alive!

He watched her backside as she strutted out the room and closed the door behind her, sealing in the darkness again.

As Stepp studied Smith's sleeping face, he wondered how many dark secrets the old man kept. He wondered how many rooms in the Vertigo Motel were occupied with this man's proverbial skeletons. How awful had this man been for Anya to have trusted him for so many decades? Had he lived a double life? A triple life even? How far had this man gone to help build the cult?

Stepp felt a sense of pride that he hadn't stooped too low for the witch. But what had that gotten him? A one-way ticket to Ghouls-ville. He absentmindedly rubbed his shirt over his chest where his heart used to be—before Anya had reached in, while he was still alive and screaming, and had ripped it right from his body, still pulsing in her hand.

Then the next thing he had remembered was being at the Vertigo. Was that where they all started? The place to face their darkest secrets before being added to her ranks of ghouls? And Stepp still wasn't sure why he had been gifted to Smith. But Stepp knew this wasn't a life he wanted to live—at least not one where he couldn't boink the hot secretaries anymore. Christ, he didn't even have the reflexes to drive his IROC anymore; what was the point of living?

No, he needed to free himself from these shackles. He couldn't be anyone's slave. And it would be a win-win. He'd be doing old man Smith a service. He'd had a nice long life. He had the wife and the kids and the grandkids. And he'd had his secret killings.

Stepp let his shaky hands hover over Smith's face. He knew if the old man died, Stepp would be relieved of this rotting coil—no more electric boogaloos for this playboy.

I hope you've made peace with yourself, old man, he thought as he clamped both palms over Smith's nose and mouth.

Detective Smith's eyes snapped open, and he bucked in the bed.

Stepp pressed harder.

Smith focused on the bantling's snarled smile and bashed Stepp's face with both fists.

Stepp did not flinch, the strikes not hurting his reanimated flesh.

Smith caught the wire to the heart monitor with one of his swings and disconnected it. The flatline beep echoed through the room.

Stepp pressed harder.

Smith tried to get any of Stepp's hand between his teeth to bite down to get him to release the pressure, but all he got was chunks of decayed flesh flaking off like a biscuit.

The door flung open, and the overheads lights turned on. Three nurses and a doctor ran into the room to see their patient flailing on the bed and gasping for breath.

Stepp pressed harder.

Two of the nurses tried to hold Smith's bucking body to the bed so the third nurse and the doctor could assess the situation and could start medical intervention.

Smith kicked both legs and swung his arms wildly at the murderous ghoul pinning him.

"Hold him down!" the doctor ordered and grabbed a bag valve mask.

"We're trying!"

"His heart monitor fell off," the third nurse said, noticing the dangling wire.

Stepp pressed harder.

"He's not breathing!" one of the nurses holding him down said.

The doctor hovered over Smith's face and tried to pinch his nose to start CPR. "I can't grab his nose." He stood, dumbfounded.

"What do you mean, you can't?"

"You try!"

The nurse switched positions with the doctor and tried to pinch closed Smith's nose. She was met with the same invisible resistance just above his nose.

Stepp grinned as the doctor and the nurse with the cute ass had tried to perform CPR, but his hand covering Smith's nose and mouth acted as a barrier.

The doctor tried to place the bag valve mask over Smith's face, but the mask just stopped inches over his face.

Stepp watched the doctor press the bag valve mask on the back of Stepp's hand and laughed. He contemplated materializing, as his final stroke of comedy, just to see the looks on their faces. He felt Smith's struggle wane under the pressure of his hands.

"We're losing him. Do something!" one of the nurses yelled.

"I … I don't know … what's going on," the doctor said and stepped backward from the bed.

Stepp knew Smith had only seconds left before he passed on, and, with Smith leaving this plane, Stepp knew he would go too, as he had been a gift to the detective by his re-maker.

Smith's muscles relaxed, and his eyes drooped, and his limbs' flailings turned to light slaps and haphazard movements. This was the end, and Stepp knew it—the end for both of them.

Stepp pressed harder. He stared at Smith's eyes as his pupils dilated, and his head slumped to the side on the pillow, his limbs falling hard against the bedside railings.

Stepp materialized and used the fraction of a second he knew he had left in his existence to hiss at the three nurses and doctor, hoping to make this moment define every nightmare for the rest of their stupid lives.

The nurses and doctor scrambled backward from the zombie that had just appeared in the room.

Stepp glanced one more time at the now-deceased Detective Smith, the ex–Wharf Killer, before he felt nothingness consume him, and he was met with a black void, and all his thoughts ceased.

LAS VEGAS, NEVADA; 1984

18: HEADLESS

Melissa jolted awake in a panic, like she was late for the school bus. She surveyed the room and remembered where she was and what was happening. The sun peeked through the slats in the blinds, and she heard a sizzling noise coming from somewhere in the house. She padded across the guestroom floor and entered the hallway. "Uncle Hank?"

"Down here, love. Got bacon in the pan."

"Smells great." Melissa traipsed into the kitchen and sat at the counter.

"Want some coffee? Wait. Are you allowed to have coffee?"

"I would love some. And, yes, I'm allowed to have it."

Hank turned for the carafe, and Melissa giggled at his white bunny slippers and pink robe. "I heard you have lunch plans with Floyd's granddaughter today?"

She shifted uncomfortably on the stool. "Yah. I kinda got sucked into it, but she seemed pretty excited."

Hank turned to fill an ancient coffee mug that read TOP REPORTER FOR HIRE and handed it to her. "Be gentle with her, love. She's … special."

"Oh, I got that, Uncle." Melissa chuckled and sipped her coffee. "I'm afraid she'll be eaten alive next year in high school."

"Bullies will be bullies."

"Yeah, but that's no excuse."

"You, love, are wise beyond your years. I just wish you had been wise enough not to run away across country."

Melissa sighed. She had been so consumed with Laura and Anya and Scarlet that she had forgotten about her real life—the one where her parents were coming to collect her and then the possible repercussions she faced back home. Even though she felt like she was finally on the good side of the fight, there was still a dead secretary because of her. "I was being stupid. I know I've learned my lesson."

"You always were a smart girl. And your parents are fair. I'm sure y'all will work it out."

Melissa took another sip of coffee and lowered the mug halfway to the counter to look at its typeset. "Do you ever miss being a reporter?"

Hank sat across from her, opened a packet of cocoa mix, and dumped it into his coffee. "It's been a while since I could honestly say I miss those times. A lot of good things came from that job. That's how I met your grandfather. He was a cop, still working the beat, and I was a go-getter reporter for the local newspaper. We became fast friends." He took a long sip and closed his eyes. "Your grandpa sometimes went undercover, using the name Todd Arbuckle. That was a long time ago though. Feels like someone else lived that life now."

"Grandpapa has the same mug, but his says *Gun* instead of *Reporter*. I drink hot chocolate from it sometimes." She eyed the cocoa packet on the counter for dramatic effect.

"Your grandmother made that mug for him. I liked it so much that I had one made for myself."

"That's ... kind of sad, Uncle."

"Well, I didn't really have that someone special for most of my life."

"But you had one, right?"

Hank sighed. "Olli. Again, so long ago that it seems like someone else's story."

"Do tell!" Melissa leaned back slightly to show she was getting comfortable for a long tale.

"Nothing to tell really." Hank paused for an emphysemic coughing fit. "I think he maybe got bored with me and flew the coop."

A swirl of red and blue flashed behind Melissa's eyes, and she found herself standing in a long hallway, with multiple doors on either side. Instead of fear and confusion, she walked forward with confidence. She didn't understand how she knew to stop in front of this particular door, but she did. She gripped the doorknob and paused.

"Open it," a man said, standing in the hallway a few doors down. "In the Vertigo, all secrets are revealed. Don't be afraid."

Melissa released the knob and turned toward the man with no face—it was like smooth white clay and devoid of features—wearing a train conductor uniform. "No. Some secrets are better left buried."

"You only come to the Vertigo to unearth those secrets," he growled. "If you refuse"—he approached rapidly—"then why are you here?"

"I-I didn't mean to come here."

"Behind that door!" He pointed at the door. "Behind that door! Behind that door! Behind that door! Behind that door!"

Melissa stepped backward. "I don't want to know!"

The faceless man grabbed her arm. "But you came here to know! Came to the Vertigo to know! To know! To know what happened! What happened! What happened behind that door! Behind that door! Behind that door!"

Melissa closed her eyes and clamped both hands over ears. "I don't want to know!"

Blue and red lights flashed, and she caught herself as she fell backward off the stool.

"Oh, jeepers. Are you okay, love?" Hank ambled around the counter to help set her upright again on the stool.

She shook the cobwebs from her brain. "Yeah, I'm fine. Just got a little dizzy. I'm fine now."

Hank nodded and returned to his spot across from her.

She eyed him wearily, unaware she had experienced her first taste of the Vertigo Motel, and wondered what had really happened between Hank and Olli.

Hank brought a handkerchief to his mouth so he could cough into it. "My lungs will be the death of me. Mark my words."

"Oh, Uncle. You can't go anywhere just yet. Who would serve the tastiest tacos in all of Vegas if you died?"

"Flattery will get you nowhere, love."

"Unless I'm Floyd?"

Hank furrowed his brows at her. "Touché. But is it that obvious?"

"That you want to jump his bones? Yes."

"Child! Language!"

Melissa cringed at Hank calling her the same term of endearment that Anya favored.

"Well, we should get ready. Your parents are landing later today, and you don't want to be late for your picnic. I just want to thank you for doing this with Scarlet."

"Why are you thanking me?"

"Because I think it's earning me some bonus points with Floyd."

Melissa jokingly slammed her coffee mug on the counter. "Oh, so now you're using me to get in with your buddy."

"Oh, you shush!" Hank exploded into a coughing fit, and he covered his mouth in the crook of his elbow.

Melissa swiveled off the stool. "I'm going to shower. Let me know when we're leaving."

Hank recovered and watched Melissa head out of the kitchen. "I love you, Mel."

"I love you too, Uncle Hank."

The car bounced along the road as Melissa rested her hands on the cooler of food for the picnic.

Hank turned into the shared parking lot of the two restaurants, parked in front of the Taco Shed's front doors, and killed the engine. "You sure you want to bring those cold cuts to the picnic? I can whip up some burritos and tacos that will knock off your knickers."

Melissa chuckled. "Thanks, but I think these will do fine. To go along with the sandwiches, I have some Tab soda and Keebler Magic Middles that I found in your pantry." She hoped Hank wouldn't want to inspect the food in the cooler.

It had proved difficult to hide the rope that she had grabbed from Hank's garage underneath the food.

"I think she's more excited than you." Hank pointed through the windshield.

Melissa saw Scarlet bounding through the Castaway's front door toward the car, smiling and waving. "Oh God …"

"Be nice. It's just one lunch. And it might mean a lot on the other end."

Melissa saw Hank's face light up as he stepped from the car to greet Floyd, who was crossing the parking lot.

"Hey, girlfriend!" Scarlet greeted as Melissa exited the car. "Ready for our picnic?"

Melissa swallowed hard and took a deep breath. "Totally ready." She raised the cooler chest high. "I hope you like turkey and cheese."

"Love it. And I have some music for you to hear." Scarlet pulled a small, one-speaker boombox halfway from her backpack.

"Gonna be a great time."

"Don't stay out too long," Floyd said to his granddaughter. "You know that desert sun is a killer. But you girls have fun."

Scarlet waved goodbye, and the two girls traversed the parking lot.

"It's pretty easy to get to. We just follow this road until we hit the desert," Scarlet said as they turned left onto the main road.

Melissa switched hands holding the cooler during the walk, mulling over what was about to transpire in the desert. She played out every scenario in her head, from them defeating Anya to Anya killing everyone.

"Did you even hear anything I said?" Scarlet asked.

207 Headless | 207

"Huh?"

"I knew you weren't paying attention. I said I've been thinking about how cool you are and how much confidence you give me."

"Uh-huh …"

"So, I think I want to dye my hair purple."

"Dying your hair isn't what will make you cool. Being you and owning it, that's what makes you hip." Melissa wiped a coat of sweat from her forehead. "Look. You're weird. But that makes you unique. Be weird. Just be you."

Scarlet nodded once. "This is why you're my best friend."

Melissa took a regretful breath as they turned from the roadway and entered the sand and scattered cacti of the desert.

"My spot is just up there." Scarlet pointed to where two cacti seemed to be leaning into each other.

Melissa had to lift her feet higher than normal to clear the uneven topography of the sand. She thought how nice it would have been if Scarlet had offered just once to switch, so she would carry the lightweight backpack with the boombox and Scarlet would carry the heavy cooler full of food and soda—but, no, of course that wouldn't have dawned on her. Because she was Scarlet.

Scarlet stopped and smiled at Melissa, and Melissa knew they had reached their picnic spot—even though she couldn't figure what made *this* spot more special than the repeating landscape of sand and nothingness. She let the cooler drop from her fingers in frustration and exhaustion instead of lowering it to the sand.

"Did you bring a blanket or something to sit on?" Scarlet asked.

"You gotta be kidding me," Melissa said through gritted teeth. "I thought this was your special spot. Why didn't you bring whatever you would normally come with?"

"Oh, I don't usually eat here. Or have a friend with me."

"Of course you don't," Melissa mumbled.

Scarlet reached for the cooler lid.

Melissa slapped her hand away and hastily sat on the cover, preventing Scarlet from opening it. "So … *uh*, you said you brought some music for me to listen to? Maybe we could do that first?" *I just need a few more minutes to settle my nerves before all hell breaks loose.*

Scarlet removed the one-speaker boombox from her backpack and set it on the sand. "This one is called 'The Marriage of Figaro' by Amadeus. You know how some people warm up before they do aerobics?"

"You mean, like Jazzercise?"

"Exactly. So, this song is my warmup, to keep me focused, to relax to work on my poems."

"You need … a warmup to relax?"

"See? I knew you got me. We really are best friends."

Melissa shook her head and drew a small line in the sand with the toe of her sneaker, trying to put her nervous energy somewhere.

Scarlet retrieved a purple Trapper Keeper—adorned with wolves howling at the Northern Lights—from her backpack, opened it, and three composition journals fell to the sand. "Oh, clumsy me!"

Just play the fucking song so we can get this over with.

Scarlet collected her scattered poetry journals, tucked them under one armpit, and pressed Play on the boombox. Over the speaker, some woman sounded like she was wailing about something to do with a war. Scarlet's eyes widened, and she stepped backward.

Melissa laughed so hard that she had to bend forward and put her hands on her knees. "You should have seen your face!"

Scarlet's expression grew serious. "Do you know who that was?"

"Pat Benatar. 'Love is a Battlefield'."

"My mom must have left one of her tapes in it." She quickly hit Eject and removed the white cassette. "Great. Now I can't play Amadeus for you. I wish she'd stop swapping my tapes for her music to play at her lunchtime cocktail parties."

Melissa watched Scarlet clench the cassette so hard that her knuckles turned white. "Settle down there, killer. I'm sure we can have a picnic without Figaro."

"She's always ruining my life!" Scarlet kicked a divot of sand into the air and chucked the cassette, like a frisbee, against a cactus.

Melissa became hyper-focused as she slowly opened the top of the cooler. It was time to fire the proverbial shot that hopefully would be heard around the netherworld. Her fingers found the rope. She secured it with a clenched fist, narrowed her gaze at her target, and inhaled as much breath and courage as her body could hold. She charged forward like a bull and struck Scarlet's diaphragm with her shoulder.

The girl grunted as they hit the sand. "What the—"

Melissa clamped a hand over the girl's mouth and lowered her face so they were nose to nose. "Do *not* yell. This won't take long, and you'll be fine, I promise, but I need you to not run away."

Scarlet tried to escape Melissa's fingers so she could create space to scream for help.

Melissa jammed a knee into Scarlet's thigh to make the girl curl into a ball so she could bind her legs with the rope, now allowing Scarlet to scream bloody murder. Once her legs were fastened together, Melissa felt like she was playing patty-cake with Scarlet's flailing arms, trying to still them long enough to tie the rope around her wrists.

Scarlet wiggled left and right, like a worm, and screamed so loudly that Melissa thought she'd heard the girl's vocal cords tear.

Melissa scanned the empty roadway in the distance. Unless hikers were out here, she supposed the girl could scream, and no one would hear her. She straddled the girl and pivoted her head left and right. "Anya! I'm going to kill the Chosen One. I'm ending this now! You and your army of twats can go to Hell forever."

Scarlet landed a good knee-kick upward.

Melissa lost her balance and tumbled off the girl and into the sand. She grabbed Scarlet's shirt as the girl rolled over to try to get to her feet. "Anya! She dies in thirty seconds." Melissa kneeled behind Scarlet, put the girl's head in her lap, and pinched her nose closed while applying pressure to her chin to keep her mouth closed.

Scarlet bucked and twisted, but Melissa had a good center of gravity and the perfect angle, where Scarlet couldn't stabilize herself enough to wrench free.

"Time's ticking! Your Chosen One is about to say nighty-night. And I don't fucking care anymore!"

Melissa caught movement in her peripheral vision and turned to see Anya flying at her like a spear, all three rows of fangs bared. She braced for the impact as adrenaline filled her veins.

A large figure abruptly knocked the witch's trajectory midair.

Melissa raised her chin to get a better look at the two people rolling around in the sand.

"Bridgett! Now!" Baron yelled.

The Chosen One emerged from the netherworld and strode to where Baron was using an invisibility trap spell to keep Anya locked to the sand.

The witch snarled and snapped her rows of fangs at them. "I'm going to kill all three of you."

Baron rose to his feet and stood beside Hapney.

"I see you mended that cunt's wounds." Anya glared at Baron, then looked at Melissa.

"This young lady has been redeemed. You no longer have any power over her," Baron said.

Anya lunged forward and swung an arm at them, but the invisible cell kept her locked in place. She focused on the tied-up Chosen One still lying on the ground; sand had matted her hair and had stuck her tears to her face.

Melissa was surprised Scarlet hadn't resumed screaming, now that nothing was gagging her mouth. She kneeled beside the girl. "I'm going to untie you now. You can either run back home and tell a story no one will ever believe—in turn, making you even weirder to the high-schoolers you want to impress so much next year and possibly becoming the butt of every joke for the next four years—or you can go home and never speak of what you saw here."

Scarlet nodded.

Melissa untied the knots, and Scarlet stood, wiping off the clumped sand on her clothes and on her face.

"I've seen her before," Scarlet said, pointing at Anya with no sign of fear.

"You have? Where?"

"Last night. I thought I was dreaming. I woke up in the middle of the night to pee, and I thought I saw her standing behind me in the mirror when I was washing my hands."

"Makes sense. She was tailing you."

"Come here, child. I won't bite." Anya waved toward Scarlet. She opened her mouth, and all her rows of fangs retracted. "See? I put those nasty things away. I only use them on people who are trying to hurt me."

"Do it, Bridgett," Baron said in just above a whisper.

Hapney stepped between Baron and Anya, and Anya cackled.

"You have no power over me, you shrew. Only the Chosen One and I share that connection." Anya glanced at Scarlet.

Hapney reached into her pocket and rubbed her hag stone. She closed her eyes so she could visualize the words of the death spell before she attempted to speak them.

"What is this? Some kind of circus sideshow?" Anya chortled and mockingly thumbed at Hapney, then spoke to Scarlet. "Come here, child. I can make you the most popular girl at school next year."

Scarlet stepped forward.

"Don't listen to her!" Melissa extended her arm as a barrier.

"I can make even the cheerleaders envious of you. I can make you Homecoming Queen. Prom Queen. It's all right here for you."

Melissa felt pressure on her arm-bar as Scarlet inched forward toward the witch. Melissa grabbed Scarlet by both shoulders and looked into her eyes. "She's lying. She's a fucking witch!"

"Oh. My. God. Like, from Salem? Like, a real witch?" Scarlet's demeanor went from one almost hypnotized to one of a girl at a Michael Jackson concert.

"That's right, child. Come to Auntie Anya." The witch kicked the invisible prison. "As you can see, your friends have it so I can't come to you." She slowly raised the black veil to expose her pale face. "*I'm* your friend, dearest Scarlet."

"Dammit, Madam! What's taking you so long?" Melissa yelled.

"Don't rush me! I only have one chance at this!"

"What's that bitch going on about?" Anya asked. Then her eyes widened, and she stepped backward. "*You! You're* the Chosen One?" The witch made a violent arm swing, like throwing a baseball as far as she could. "Fuck me! This whole time?" she snarled, and all three rows of fangs reappeared. "You …" She pointed at Baron. "You kept her hidden. I'm going to eat both of you, throw you back up, then eat you again."

Hapney started reciting the death spell, her heart pounding. The ancient language rolled off her tongue like she was saying her own name. The faster she spoke, the more fluid the syllables sounded.

Anya reached for her own face as her skin boiled and popped. Large lesions of flesh bubbled until they exploded, spraying blood and purple ooze onto the desert sand. The skin on the backs of her hands slid off, as if she were a vampire trapped in the sunlight. She screamed as loud as she could, and the first row of fangs fell from her gums.

Hapney spoke with confidence and in an even pace, relishing the sounds of the witch's dying wails.

Melissa lowered her head but kept her eyes trained on the witch. She wanted to witness the disintegration of every molecule that comprised Anya. Mel felt Scarlet grab her hand, and the girl buried her face in Melissa's shoulder.

Anya fell to her knees, grabbed a fistful of sand, and collected herself long enough to mutter a single-syllabic word that none of them were familiar with. Then she collapsed to the sand.

Without warning, Hapney was yanked off her feet and smothered by the sand, an incredible weight pressing on her. Before the legion of ghouls could completely block out the sunlight, Mel saw Baron also overrun by the swarming bodies. Then all she saw were rotting arms and legs and decaying faces.

"Do not kill her!" Anya commanded her army, her body rejuvenating now that the death spell was no longer being spoken. "I need her alive. She's the Chosen One."

Melissa gripped Scarlet and whispered, "Now's a good time for us to run."

They turned and took one quick step forward, until Scarlet tripped over the boombox.

"Oh, and them! You can kill them," Anya said to her brood, pointing at the two girls. "And leave nothing. I don't want either of them for future use."

"Fuck, we gotta go!" Melissa yelled.

Scarlet scrambled to her feet, and Melissa now realized how difficult it was to sprint over sand.

A perfect single row of vultures descended from the sky and landed in front of the fleeing girls, creating a wall of birds that extended as far as they could see in each direction.

"There must be a million of them," Melissa mumbled and squeezed Scarlet's hand in assurance and comfort.

She looked back to see two separate mounds of ghouls, one had Hapney and the other had Baron trapped underneath. She couldn't see any part of either person through the crude pile of moving, rotting flesh. Beyond the two mounds, she watched Anya stand perfectly straight and walk forward, no longer confined by the invisible prison.

"Shit, shit, shit. Baron must have weakened too much. Don't look behind you, Scarlet. Just ... Just close your eyes."

Melissa watched Anya swipe her arm over the two mounds, and the ghouls got off their respective victim and formed ranks behind the witch. Mel noticed Laura, still looking freshly deceased—her skin wasn't nearly as gray yet—wandering around, not really sure where she was supposed to go.

When every cultist was behind the witch, Anya surveyed the two writhing figures on the sand. She kneeled beside Hapney and whispered into her ear, "You're now mine."

Hapney's contorted and disfigured body couldn't move, but her eyes watched every gesture the witch made. She took sharp, quick, fearful breaths, preparing for death, when she watched the witch stand over her body and lower the black veil. Hapney's body was so badly broken and bruised that she didn't care in what manner death came now—as long as it was swift. She was well beyond wishing for it to be painless.

The last thing she saw was Baron's hand twitch, and the last thing she thought was, *He's still alive!* before the world turned dark purple and shrunk to a pinpoint in the center of her vision, like a TV quickly turning off.

Hapney's body stretched like she was just waking up from a long nap—bones creaking and joints popping back into place—then slowly rose to her feet. Hapney's eyes glanced down at the discarded black robe and veil lying on the sand.

"Where'd she go, Mel?" Scarlet asked. "The witch, I mean."

"No, no, no … There's no way."

"What? What? Tell me …"

Melissa refused to answer. She refused to say what she thought may have happened because that might make it real. "I think we're all fucked."

Hapney's body turned to face the girls, and when she opened her mouth to speak, Melissa saw three rows of fangs. "I'm going to eat both of you, after I finally kill this piece of shit," Hapney's mouth said in Anya's voice. Then the witch-possessed psychic snatched the Mushroom Cult book from underneath the discarded robe and took a few steps toward Baron's body, crumpled on the sand.

Melissa contemplated reciting the chant that Anya had made her memorize for when it came time to sacrifice the Chosen One. She thought maybe—just maybe—if she said the chant while Anya was *inside* the Chosen One's body, it would destroy the witch too. She was reluctant to start speaking because, if this theory worked, then she'd also be killing Hapney.

Hapney's body stood over Baron and extended her arms wide, like a crucifixion, one hand holding the book. She swayed side to side and made sounds from deep in her throat.

The infinite wall of vultures also swayed in time, perfectly matching Hapney-Anya's motion.

"This isn't good," Melissa said.

"Look!" Scarlet said. "I think he's baiting her."

Melissa squinted and focused on Baron's face. She noticed his eyes were open just a slit, just enough to watch Anya without tipping her off that he was awake. As Mel studied harder, she noticed the arm he laid on was moving slowly into the trench coat he always wore. She glanced quickly behind her at the wall of vultures, checking if they had seen that she and Scarlet had noticed Baron's ruse.

Hapney-Anya closed her eyes, brought her hands together in a prayer gesture—the book between them—and raised her head as skyward as her neck would allow.

In what looked like a single blur of movement, Baron swiped both legs, connecting with Hapney's knees, and took the possessed woman to the ground in a plume of sand.

Hapney-Anya snarled as the book landed with a *thump* a few yards away.

Baron was on his feet, then had a knife blade held to Hapney's throat in what looked like one fluid motion. "Girls, I'll need your help!"

Melissa jerked Scarlet's arm forward as she took off running toward Baron. She glanced behind her at the vultures and was surprised to see them still swaying to the same tempo, as if nothing had changed. She couldn't tell if that made her feel relieved or made her feel more suspicious.

They reached Baron and Hapney-Anya, and he pointed to Anya's book. "Scarlet, you grab that book, put it in the cooler, and sit on it. We can't let her reach it. Melissa, here.

Take mine." Baron reached into his trench coat with his other hand and tossed the girl his own book.

She grabbed it from the sand and could tell the difference between the two books; this one felt heavier, even though they were the same size. Then she heard Baron's voice inside her head. *If anything happens to me, that will be yours, and your number one priority is to finish her off.*

"Careful what you say," Hapney growled in Anya's voice. "We hear everything."

Baron scrunched his face and glared at Hapney-Anya.

An invisible force pushed Hapney's body deeper against the sand. She struggled, but every inch of her backside was glued to the ground. She tried raising her head, but even that was futile. "I am going to cut—" Lip-stitches formed through her mouth, silencing her.

Baron stood and eyed the girls, Scarlet now sitting on the cooler. "I'm going to try an exorcism. This won't end pretty either way. If I can expel Anya from Bridgett's body, Bridgett will die, but so will Anya. If I fail, Anya will keep control of the Chosen One's body. She'll never become immortal, like she had planned, but trading up to a new vessel has extended her life at least another thousand years. If I fail, Mel, all my power is in that book. I want you to read the invisibility spell right now, memorize it, because if I fail, you'll need it to get out of here alive."

Melissa nodded and flipped through the book, quickly noticing all the spells were in alphabetical order—unlike Anya's Mushroom Cult book, which seemed like all the pages had been scattered, and then someone had randomly shoved them back inside.

Hapney-Anya struggled, trying to wriggle free, but the spell was too strong, and she couldn't even shift the tiniest bit from side to side.

Baron made the sign of the cross with his thumb on his forehead, then his lips, then over his heart. "Save your servant, who trusts in you, my God. Let her find in you, Lord, a fortified tower in the face of the enemy." Then Baron continued by reciting the Lord's Prayer.

Hapney-Anya screamed from behind sealed lips, and her gaze commanded him to stop.

Baron closed his eyes and recited a part of the exorcism in Latin.

Melissa had found the invisibility spell and started memorizing the simple three lines while watching Hapney-Anya fighting for any inch to gain traction on the ground.

Baron opened his eyes and screamed, "The power of Christ compels you!"

His words seemed to set off a chain reaction behind them. Melissa and Scarlet turned to the sound and saw the infinite wall of vultures had stopped swaying but were now all flapping their wings in unison.

"This doesn't seem good," Scarlet said from atop the cooler.

"No. No, it doesn't. Baron! I think we're about to have company!"

He turned to see what was happening just as a million birds of prey took flight, blackening the sky with their bodies.

Melissa instinctively covered her face for protection, and Scarlet squealed, rolling over on top of the cooler. Melissa peeked through the slits in her fingers to see Baron raise his hands in defense before the swarm of razor-sharp beaks bomb-dived his face and neck. Melissa heard a muffled scream of surprise and pain, and then silence.

The tidal wave of birds then redirected their course and disappeared sky bound, leaving Melissa and Scarlet staring at Baron and Hapney-Anya.

Baron's head was on one side of Hapney's body, and his body was slumped over the other side of her.

Scarlet gasped and hiccupped a sob. "They decapitated him!" she squeaked out.

"Fuck. This is not good." Melissa closed her eyes to start reciting the invisibility spell.

"Whatever it is you need to do, hurry it up," Scarlet said.

Melissa only opened one eye and saw Hapney's body unglued from the sand and rising to her feet. "This is doubly not good."

Hapney's mouth opened to reveal the three sets of Anya's fangs, and she moved with such cartoonish speed toward the girls that the sand kicked up behind her feet, like smoke behind a spinning tire.

"What do I do about the book in the cooler?" Scarlet yelled.

"We gotta fucking leave it! Just run!" The girls took off sprinting as Melissa belted the final line in the invisibility spell and tucked Baron's book under her arm. "If that worked, she can't hear or see us anymore. Start running in a weaving pattern so she can't guess where we are."

Scarlet ran in a snaking fashion, as if she were slaloming around cones, toward the road.

Melissa looked behind them as they ran and swerved and saw Hapney-Anya standing still, fists balled in frustration.

"I know where you're staying, you wretched child! I know where you live. I know where your family lives! I will bring slow death to everyone you love first, before I finish you off by fucking eating your soul! Do you hear me, bitch?"

"Just keep running," Melissa said quietly between panting.

"I can't believe you're a witch too," Melissa heard Scarlet mumble under her breath.

But she knew she was so, so much more than *just a witch* now.

Bridgett Hapney's vision went in reverse from when it had faded in the desert. The pinhole expanded rapidly, and she stared at a reception desk in a foyer that looked like it had just barely survived an earthquake, an apocalypse, and possibly a flood that had been allowed to naturally dry out. Gross.

As she surveyed the dilapidated area straight out of a *Twilight Zone* episode, a man wearing a gray concierge uniform came from the back room.

"*Ah*, checking in?"

"Checking in? What do you mean? Where am I?"

"You're at the Vertigo Motel, madam, of course. And you're just in luck. We only have one vacancy right now." The concierge smiled a toothless grin. "But it's a special room, one just for you."

Hapney cocked her head and reluctantly accepted the proffered keychain dangling from the man's fingers. She wrapped her fingers around the cold metal key.

The concierge pointed to a door directly across from them, one not yet in the hallway.

Her gaze followed where his finger pointed, and she took cautious steps toward it. She startled when the outline of the doorjamb burst into white light, as if the light was trying to escape through the small slits surrounding the door, then the door slid open, left to right, revealing an elevator. She stopped and glanced back at the concierge.

He straightened his bowtie and nodded.

"Where does it go?" she asked.

He brushed a plume of dust off the counter and wrote in a ledger without looking up at her again. "A special invitation to the dance."

"Wha-What dance?"

The concierge slammed the ledger closed, tucked it under an armpit, and came around the counter to stand alongside her. "A waltz, if you will, to the land of peacefulness and serenity."

"I still don't—"

"Go"—he gave her a slight nudge—"because if you don't, I will sure as hell take your spot, away from this eternal hellhole. Use that key when you get to the top."

Hapney pressed her lips together in confidence and nodded once. She approached the opened elevator, stopped when she reached it, turned to the concierge one last time, and stepped backward into the cabin.

The brightest and most-welcoming light Madam Hapney had ever felt engulfed her. The door slid shut, leaving the concierge alone in the dim and deteriorating Vertigo Motel lobby.

He didn't turn back to his post behind the counter until the very last iota of light had faded from the cracks in the doorjamb, after the cabin had lifted away from the ground floor. It was only then that he knew Madam Hapney had become one with the universe again.

19: ONLY THE HAUNTED

Travis handed the cab driver a hefty tip and slammed the rear taxi door. With one hand holding their only bag of luggage, he reached for Gwen's hand with the other. Their fingers interlaced, and they headed to Hank's front door. Travis knocked, and they waited.

The door swung open, revealing Hank's tear-stained face.

Travis dropped the bag and his wife's hand and grabbed Hank's shoulders, as if he thought the old man would pass out. "Hank, what's wrong?

Wide-eyed, Hank sniffled and shook his head. "Come. Sit with me at the table. I have tea brewing."

Travis and Gwen followed Hank through the living room and into the kitchen. They sat without being told to again and remained silent.

Hank poured three cups of tea and turned to face his best friend's family. "Travis, your father passed away sometime during the night."

Gwen gasped, and Travis silently clapped his hand over his mouth.

"Wynn called me this morning. She didn't know how else to get in touch with you guys, since you had already left for the airport when they had confirmed it."

Gwen eyed her husband to see if he would ask anything, and when he remained silent, she looked at Hank. "Do they know from what? Another heart attack?"

Hank slid two cups of tea toward them and shrugged. "They said they'll know more after the autopsy. I guess he just … stopped breathing."

"Wasn't he on a respirator?" Travis asked loudly.

Hank lowered his gaze. "I don't know the specifics, love."

Gwen rubbed Travis's forearm for comfort. "Our flight is in the morning. Not much we can do from here, except get our daughter. We'll go straight to see your mother as soon as we land."

Travis nodded and stared at his steeping tea.

"Where is Mel?" Gwen asked Hank.

He sat across from them with his own tea. "She's on a picnic with the granddaughter of the owner of the restaurant next to mine. Kind of a favor to him. She's … having a hard time keeping friends."

Travis stood so fast that his chair toppled behind him. "Our daughter somehow hitchhikes across country to your house, and you let her out of your sight the very next day to go play with a girl she doesn't know?"

"Travis," Gwen whispered. "Sit down. It's fine."

He glanced at his wife's face. "Sorry, Hank." He righted the chair and sat again. "Sorry. It's been a flood of emotions the last few days. And now. Thank you for keeping her safe and for calling us."

Hank reached across the table and patted Travis's hand. "You guys are family to me. The only family I ever had. I'm glad Mel thinks that highly of me that she would pick my place to run away to." He leaned back in his chair as a rack of coughing shook his chest.

"Please tell us that you're under a doctor's care," Gwen said. "People die from emphysema all the time."

Hank raised a single finger while he finished his coughing attack and nodded. "Maybe it wasn't the wisest choice to let Mel go out today, but I guess that's a pitfall of never having kids myself; I'm not quite sure what to do with them."

"Well, we have three, and sometimes we still don't know what to do with them," Gwen said.

Travis leaned into his wife and wiped a tear from his cheek. "I'm gonna go call Ma."

"Phone's right there." Hank pointed to the wall.

Travis rose to head to the phone and stopped when the front door flung open, and Melissa and Scarlet sprinted in like gangbusters.

The girls screamed at the adults in unison, both saying different things.

"Whoa, whoa!" Hank yelled. "One at a time!"

"Honey, are you okay?" Gwen stood from the chair and reached for her daughter.

Melissa stepped backward and wiped the sand stuck to her forehead with her sleeve of her arm that wasn't holding Baron's book. "I know this will sound crazy, but we gotta get outta here! There's a crazed, possessed, witch-demon thing after us."

Gwen chuckled and held up her hand. "While I'm glad you have a made a new friend, we have to talk to you about quite a few things."

Scarlet wiped the stinging sweat from her eyes. "She's telling the truth! And I think the zombies might be with her!"

Hank raised his eyebrows and ambled as fast as he could to close the front door. He placed a palm over his chest to try to calm his racing heart.

Melissa bolted for the guestroom, Baron's book clenched tight in her hands.

"Where are you going, young lady?" Gwen asked, using both hands to wipe tears from her eyes. "This has already been a shit morning, and we don't need you adding to the chaos!"

"To my room to get my backpack. We gotta go!" she answered while disappearing around the corner.

"Oh no you don't!" Travis said, heading after her. "Last time we let you go to your room to get something, you took off."

"I'm Scarlet," she said to Melissa's mother, now that they were the only two left in the kitchen.

"Nice to meet you." Gwen turned to the front door. "Hank? You okay? You look like you just saw a ghost."

Hank shuffled to the kitchen. "Scarlet, tell me exactly what you saw."

Scarlet got distracted by the sounds of Melissa and her father arguing loudly from the other room. "We went to my spot in the desert, where I like to write my poems, and Melissa tied me up and—"

"She *what?*" Gwen asked.

"Hold on, Mrs. Melissa. It wasn't for reals. It was to get this witch she's been huntin' or something out into the open so this other witch dude could kill her. But then she possessed this other lady, and that book—"

Gwen sarcastically laughed. "Okay, yeah, right. It's nice to meet you, Scarlet, but Mel knows how much trouble she's in. I appreciate you trying to cause a diversion for her, but it'll only get her in more trouble."

Hank watched Scarlet's face redden in frustration as she clenched her fists. Hank told Gwen, "I … I don't think she's lying."

The front door blew off its hinges behind them, and they instinctively ducked.

"That's her!" Scarlet yelled. "Mel! We gotta go!"

Hapney-Anya stepped into the foyer. "Where are they, old man?"

Scarlet's gaze darted between Hank and Melissa's mother, who had crawled under the kitchen table, her knees tucked to her chest, and started screaming.

Hank glanced to where Scarlet stood and understood, then regarded the possessed psychic. "They're not here."

Hapney-Anya floated toward Hank and stopped nose to nose.

Gwen squeaked from under the table.

"I could have, should have killed you many times over, back when you were runnin' with Smith. But I never in a million years thought you, Hank Steel, would be the human who stood between me and my destiny. Now tell me where that fucking cunt is."

Gwen's eyes widened at the mention of their last name and the manner in how this *thing* referred to her daughter. She swallowed the saliva that had built in her mouth and came out of hiding. "What do you want with my daughter?" She tucked her hands behind her back to hide their quaking; she was concerned that showing fear would be exploited against her.

Hapney-Anya's head turned slowly toward Gwen.

Scarlet stepped backward again. "Mel! She's here!"

Melissa ran into the kitchen with her backpack and Baron's book, her father in tow, and stopped when she reached the threshold.

Travis halted and gasped.

Hapney-Anya noticed Travis. "I see the family's all here. Came to pick up your little runaway? I always loved that song. I'm not going to ask this again. Where *the fuck* are they?"

"Dad, if you only trust me once for the rest of my life, you need to trust me now. She can't hear or see me and Scarlet. I'll explain later."

Travis's breath remained hitched in his lungs.

"Tell her that you're here, waiting for me and Scarlet to return, so you can take me home."

Travis stayed silent and motionless.

"Say it, Dad!"

His eyes darted to his daughter.

"Don't look at me! She knows she can't see us. You'll give me away!"

Hapney-Anya stepped away from Hank and Gwen and approached the doorway. She swiped a hand toward the space where Travis had looked.

Melissa ducked under the witch's arm, ran into the kitchen, and turned to watch the witch swipe again at empty air.

"Nobody look at us when we talk. She can't hear or see us. I need, like, fifteen seconds to put the spell over all of us." She lowered herself to the floor so she could prop open the book on her knee to find the page again.

Travis released a muffled wail as Hapney's hand clenched his throat.

She brought her lips to his ear. "Point. To. Where. They. Are."

Gwen sobbed and let out an "Oh God ... please, help." She shuffled backward to the knife rack on the counter.

Melissa put her finger to her lips, and Scarlet nodded, surprisingly calm, now knowing they were still invisible.

"Point, you fucker!" Hapney-Anya ordered.

Travis closed his eyes so he wouldn't inadvertently look at either his daughter or her friend. He kept both arms steeled against his side.

Hapney-Anya squeezed harder. "Your father was the Wharf Killer for all these years. Did you know that? Did you know"—she let her cracked and bloodied lips graze his earlobe—"you are a descendant of one of the most gruesome serial killers to ever walk the Earth?"

Gwen felt the counter hit her back, and she knew she was inches from securing a knife into her hands.

Travis pursed his lips, refusing to show any signs of acknowledgment of anything being said to him.

"And your daughter, someone who also has his sinful blood running through their veins, has found it quite easy to fill his shoes."

Gwen used her fingertips to coax the knife handle from the rack.

Melissa was now on the second line of the invisibility spell, Scarlet trying to read along to herself while peering over her shoulder.

"Where is your daughter, before I kill you, then your wife." Hapney-Anya turned her head slightly to peer at Gwen, then flew like a rocket across the kitchen. She slapped Gwen's hand off the knife handle. "Really? A knife?"

Gwen choked on the smell of the demon's rotting breath.

Travis sucked in a lungful of oxygen now that his throat was freed.

Melissa froze and stared at the newly scribed words on the page that hadn't been there when she had read the spell in the desert. Her eyes widened when she understood their meaning.

"Why'd you stop reading?" Scarlet asked.

"*Huh*? Oh, nothing," Melissa answered and resumed reciting the spell.

Hank pulled out a chair to sit, gasping for air, and took a chance to peek at Melissa and Scarlet on the floor by his feet, listening to Melissa recite the unusual words.

Hapney-Anya manhandled the knife that Gwen had attempted to grab and stepped behind Hank in the chair. She looked down at the top of his balding head and placed the knife handle between both palms.

Hank looked up at the witch disguised in someone's possessed body and couldn't dig deep enough through his labored breaths and damaged lungs to protest or fight anymore. He closed his eyes and waited for that pale death to strike.

"Tell me where she is, or he dies." The witch raised the blade above Hank's head and held it midair.

Travis quickly calculated the distance between him and the crazed woman and deducted it was too far. He knew the moment he made any twitch toward her, she would bring down the knife. He was too far away to clear that distance in time. Better to stay planted and to keep brainstorming. He had to will his gaze not to check on his daughter on the floor, reading a foreign language out loud from the old-looking book.

"We're telling the truth! They're not here!" Gwen screamed in a half cry.

"Then he dies."

The final word of the spell left Melissa lips, then she screamed, "Scarlet! Get Hank!"

Scarlet and Melissa simultaneously tackled Hank out of the chair as the witch brought down the knife like a pendulum and struck nothingness.

"You bitch!" Hapney-Anya screamed as she spun around and around in the kitchen, looking for any trace of the three people who had just been here a second ago.

"Everyone out the front door!" Melissa yelled.

Hank crawled a few steps forward before standing so he wouldn't accidentally get sliced by the knife the witch was still swinging around.

They headed for the empty doorframe, Travis's arm around Hank's shoulders to help him sputter along. They stumbled onto the sidewalk, and Melissa looked back through the doorless entryway. "She's not stupid. She'll know we left the house. We gotta keep moving."

"Are you okay?" Travis asked Gwen.

"I-I don't even know what to say right now."

"Where do we go?" Scarlet asked.

"Somewhere she won't think of. Somewhere she doesn't associate us with. Uncle Hank, any suggestions?"

"Shouldn't we get Scarlet back home?" Gwen asked. "Or call her parents?"

Hapney-Anya bolted through the front doorway and stopped. "Can you hear me, child? I'm going to find you, and

I'm going to eat all of you. I won't stop hunting you until you're all fucking dead! You'll never sleep again!" She bent backward at the waist and cackled.

"No time, Mom." Melissa shook her head. "Uncle? Anywhere?"

"Hold on, love. I'm thinking."

"How long does this invisibility spell last?" Scarlet asked. "I mean, we can't stay invisible forever, right?"

Melissa's eyes widened in realization. "But *people* can still see us! It's only Anya who can't. If it lasts forever, then, yes, I guess we keep it on forever."

"Wouldn't you be scared that she might figure out a spell to reverse it or find one that allows her to see through it?"

"Blasted. I didn't think of that."

"Let's keep moving while we talk," Travis said, supporting Hank again as they moved down the sidewalk. "Are you gonna make it?"

Hank eyed Travis. "A wise man once said, 'Life is a ride.'"

"Oh, yeah?" Travis chortled. "Who said that?"

"Your father. A long, long time ago." Hank tapped Melissa on the arm. "I know where she would never think to look …" He bent forward in a coughing fit.

Melissa walked backward so she could keep Hapney-Anya in her sights as they moved away. "Where?"

Hank composed himself and cleared his throat. "George Covington's backwoods."

"You mean …"

"Yes, where Anya killed Rose. Your grandfather said, after that happened, she treated that land like it was a repellent. I think she's scared of it."

"I don't know what the hell is going on or what the hell you are talking about, but there will be *a lot* of honest discussions behind closed doors when this is over," Travis said and looked at Hank. "*All* of us."

"We gotta hurry," Scarlet said.

Melissa diverted her gaze from the witch still standing in the doorway to her friend. "Why's that?"

"The zombies are back."

Melissa spun to face forward and saw the Mushroom Cult heading toward them.

"Now what in the hell are *those*?" Gwen asked, putting her arm protectively around Melissa's shoulders.

"They can't see us either," Melissa said. "They're probably heading for Anya. Just don't let them bump into you. Then they'll know where we are."

They stepped onto the shoulder of the road, off the sidewalk, and watched the brood shamble past them, heading for Hank's house.

Melissa noticed Laura had taken the lead.

"The only thing I'm afraid of is the vultures can see us. But they're supposed to remain neutral to all this."

"Yeah? They weren't neutral back in the desert when they created that wall of death!" Scarlet said.

"I still haven't quite figured them out yet."

"How far away is this place we're going?" Travis asked.

"About a mile," Hank answered.

"We should just get Scarlet home and get on a plane as soon as possible," Gwen said.

"She knows where I live—she appeared in my bathroom mirror, Mrs. Melissa—but if I'm protected by the spell …"

"Even if she can't see you, she'll torture your family until they give you up." Melissa countered.

"You're talking like you know this woman," Travis said. "I just can't wrap my head around all this. Dad was the Wharf Killer?" he whispered to himself.

"I do know her, Dad. Right now, we need to get to the woods so we can sit and talk this through."

They walked in silence, Hank's house with the witch and the army of ghouls fading behind them in the distance.

"What are we gonna do when we get there?" Scarlet whispered to Melissa.

"I just need a few minutes of time where everyone feels safe and can be calm."

"What is it you're not telling me? You saw something in the book when you stopped reading. I saw it on your face."

Melissa hugged Baron's book to her chest. "He left me a message."

20: END OF THE ROAD

Hank led them down the driveway that ran along the old Covington property. "The house is still in the family's name. Nothing's been done to it in years. Sometimes I think Floyd wants it to fall to the ground and be forgotten, along with the memories."

"So, what exactly happened here?" Travis asked, surveying the woods ahead. "And who's Floyd?"

"A little girl was burned while tied to a tree," Melissa said. "That … woman back there did it, thinking the girl was something else."

"Floyd is the restaurant owner next to me that I told you is Scarlet's grandfather. Rose was his niece. Her father was the Boulevard Killer."

Melissa stopped and placed a hand over her mouth.

"You okay?" Gwen asked.

"I can still see the burn marks on the tree!" Tears welled in her eyes.

Hank trudged closer to the tree line. "*Ay-yup*. Was a terrible year for us out here. Business was good for me though. Lots of stories to cover for the paper. Kept me hoppin'."

Melissa approached the scorched tree and touched the bark. "I feel like I can still sense her here. Like, her aura."

Hank stopped and turned to her. "It's possible. They say tragic deaths leave behind the most residual energy. I couldn't imagine being seven years old and burning on a tree."

Scarlet stopped beside Melissa to look at the tree too. "You know a lot about this witch's history."

Melissa sighed and squeezed Baron's book. "More than I'd like, yes."

"A clearing is right up there, through the trees," Hank said.

They followed him, breaking dead branches and crunching on small shrubbery as they advanced.

Melissa took a moment to think about the little girl she had never met but knew so much about—had thrown the girl's murder in Anya's face countless times. She couldn't believe she was standing in the spot where it had happened. She cleared the fogginess from her brain and followed her family to the clearing.

"Okay, love. We're here. Now what?"

"Well, Uncle Hank, I'm not quite sure what to expect, but I know I need to read a passage from this book. Anything could happen, but I don't think anything bad. So, whatever starts to happen, please just let it."

"I've given up trying to make sense of anything," Gwen said and hugged her daughter.

A tree branch crackled when it bent as a vulture perched on it.

"They found us, Mel," Scarlet said and pointed.

Travis stepped toward Melissa. "Now what?"

"I … I don't think the vulture will hurt us," Melissa said, keeping her gaze on the single vulture. "They usually send just one as a scout, but I don't think he'll report back to Anya. I feel … I feel he's just curious."

Travis wagged a finger at Melissa for a moment and pursed his lips. "This is ludicrous, Mel. Who *are* you?" He eyed Hank. "Ya know, if you weren't such a longtime family friend, and if I didn't trust you with my life, I wouldn't be going along with *any* of this."

Hank snickered and mumbled, "Then you'd already be dead."

"I promise to tell you everything once we get out of this, Daddy. Okay?"

Travis scrunched his face as tears dripped from his eyes. "Okay, baby. I trust you." He embraced her in a hug, then pulled back quickly when the vulture took flight and descended.

They watched it land in front of Rose's tree in the distance.

Melissa squinted to watch it clearer. "It's just looking at the tree."

"Maybe it feels guilt," Hank said.

"I don't think they can feel, not like we do. They stick to a strict set of rules, but I don't believe they make decisions based on emotions."

Hank nodded, then covered his mouth as he coughed.

Melissa opened the book to the page where she had seen the new passage. The calligraphy was shiny and gold, unlike the listless writing that adorned every other page.

Scarlet peered over Melissa's shoulder to look at the words.

"Maybe you should sit with them." Melissa gestured to her parents and Hank, who were sitting on a fallen log.

Scarlet nodded. "Right. Good idea."

Melissa waited for her newfound friend to sit, then started reading Baron's passage at just above a murmur. The vulture cocked its head as a whirlpool of wind swirled around Melissa, collecting loose debris from the ground. Melissa recited the final word in the new passage, and tendrils of light shot from her body in an explosion.

The book disintegrated in her hands, and the crumbs and particles that used to be Baron's spell book catapulted into her chest area and dissolved into her flesh. She levitated off the ground as orange flashes consumed her vision.

Anya didn't know where the little tramp had taken everyone, but she would check every damn location she could think of. She wouldn't eat until she found them. She wouldn't sleep until she found them. She wouldn't even breathe until she found them.

Hapney-Anya and her army of ghouls flashed through the netherworld into Steel's Taco Shed. She hastily transformed into Eva and flagged down the same worker she had spoken to from last time. "Excuse me, but is the owner available?"

"No, I'm sorry, ma'am. He's not due to come in today. Something about his family visiting," Joel said.

Eva smiled while growling under her breath. "Thank you." She turned to leave.

"Is there a message I can give him?"

"Not necessary," she said without stopping on her way out.

As soon as she was outside, she jumped through the netherworld again to materialize at the park with the chess tables. She grinned when she saw a man speaking to no one and gesturing animatedly with his hands. "Gotch'ya," she whispered.

Donning the Eva flesh-suit again, she strode through the park toward the man, her girls in perfect rows behind her. "Excuse me, sir. Do you know these people you're talking to?"

The man stopped talking to the invisible people and faced Anya. He smiled, revealing a top row of missing teeth. "Yes, mum. These are my new friends."

"Really?" She overexaggerated her smile and looked at the empty space where the man had been speaking to.

"Can you see them too, mum?" he asked.

"Oh, yes …" she snarled. "I can see every one of their wretched faces." She scanned the nothingness in front of her, hoping her gaze was meeting their eyes with intimidation.

"Could you tell that one to stop talking so much when I'm trying to sleep?" The man pointed at an empty space.

Anya looked at him. "What?"

"That one there. The old-timey guy with the sifter thing. He babbles on and on every night about finding gold."

Anya let Eva's shoulders slump and, with a flat tone, asked, "You see an old gold rush guy?"

"Yep. And an astronaut. And a pirate. And a lil' mouse I named Jimmy Jazz-Hands."

Anya shook Eva's head and disappeared into the netherworld to head to the next possible location.

Hapney-Anya flopped back on her throne, exhausted and discouraged from coming up empty at each place she thought to look. The problem was, Melissa might have been at any of the locations, but Anya wouldn't have known it, unless she noticed someone acting like they were either walking around people who were there or were talking to people she couldn't see.

She held a hand in front of her face to survey Hapney's limb and nodded in satisfaction. "This coil will do for a while."

Laura wobbled into the throne room, followed by a handful of ghouls.

"I don't know, ladies. Everything got so messed up. I'm at a loss." Anya relaxed one of Hapney's legs over the armrest of the throne and bounced her foot. An apple appeared in her hand, and she took a large bite. "We might just have to write off that bitch as a lost cause and get back to square one," she said, munching a mouthful of fruit. "There'll be another Chosen One. Granted, it might be one thousand years later, but there's always another one. And, as a curator for you peeps"—she swallowed the apple—"no more self-righteous detectives or whiny teenage girls. We do this the right way. We groom someone with no moral compass."

The Mushroom Cult's demeanors lightened from morose to giddy. Even the bantling Laura got caught up in the excitement, clapping and bouncing and chirping.

Anya swung Hapney's leg off the throne's armrest and stood valiantly, arched her back slightly, like an army general giving orders, and lifted both hands in the air. "Salvation lives only through me!" Hapney-Anya, unable to move her raised arms, was in shock. "How in the Devil's red Hell did you get in here?"

The army of ghouls turned to look at the entranceway, and Laura snarled. The wind inside the throne room spun counterclockwise so fast that all their shabby and tattered clothes were now stiff, perpendicular to the floor. Hapney's hair stood straight sideways, and Hapney-Anya gripped the back of her throne, fighting to be pulled sideways from the gale.

Melissa opened both hands, her palms facing the Hapney-Anya hybrid on the throne step. Mel concentrated, as if she were trying to move a small object, but, this time, the release came as effortlessly as if she had blown a feather out of the air.

Hapney's body spun end over end and slammed into the far wall, stuck upside down, like a fly on flypaper.

Laura, hissing and chomping her teeth together, lunged for the teenager.

Melissa's gaze quickly darted in Laura's direction, and the bantling was ripped apart, limbs and torso and head flying in different directions.

A collective gasp came from the rest of the cult as they huddled together, shaking, like scared puppies.

Hapney-Anya cackled from her spot on the wall. "Oh, child. You are so fucking *funny*! Nice parlor trick, witch wannabe."

Melissa walked past the trembling group of remaining ghouls who had now made a circle with their bodies, holding on to each other's shoulders for comfort. She flicked her index finger once.

Every member of the Mushroom Cult's skin melted. Thinning and fraying hair slid off their skulls; bones turned to goo; disconnected eyeballs rolled off the piles of pudding-like slop, and small bone fragments came to rest atop the mound of what used to be an army. The thick slurry of dissolved muscle, tissue, and chunks of unidentifiable body parts slowly spread outward to cover the throne room floor.

Hapney-Anya's eyes widened. "You fucking runt! You will replace every single one of those girls!" She strained to pull any part of her backside from the wall. "Are you listening to me? Can you hear the words coming out of my mouth? You will build me a new army before I destroy you!"

Melissa continued her slow approach, the tornado of wind keeping her dead center within it, even as she moved. She outstretched her right arm toward the witch's throne, locked her elbow, then splayed her fingers, her palm facing the chair. Her sweatshirt sleeve pulled back slightly, with her arm fully extended, exposing her wrist. Anya's throne exploded in a shower of splintered wood and torn silk.

Hapney-Anya cringed when the throne vaporized, but then she noticed Melissa's wrist. She strained even harder to frantically peel herself off the wall. She screamed into the oncoming windstorm that slowly traversed her throne room. She screamed so loud that Hapney's vocal cords cracked, and only air pushed through her mouth.

Melissa silently stayed the course toward the witch's upside-down stolen body. Nothing left to destroy now—except the evil in front of her.

Hapney-Anya stopped screaming. "Sweetie, please. I'll do anything. Just ... Just don't kill me. You've destroyed the cult.

You blew up my throne. Take the netherworld for yourself if you want. Just spare me. Just … have a little mercy. Please."

Melissa paused, taken aback by the witch's tone change. Then she noticed Hapney's gaze dart ever-so-slightly to Melissa's exposed wrist. She turned over her arm and saw a tattoo of a triangle with a single eye in the center on her wrist—Baron's book and everything he was and everything he knew was a physical part of her. She realized she didn't need to memorize anything anymore; she innately *knew* it. And this petrified the witch enough to grovel.

Melissa restarted her trek forward again, keeping the swirling gale moving in time with her steps toward the witch.

"Fucking say something!" Hapney-Anya screamed at her. "Can't we just talk this out? God alive, I couldn't get you to shut up before. Now you won't give me the decency to answer me? I was saving you! Me! No one else. I was giving you a pathway to freedom. Me!"

Melissa stopped in front of the upside-down body of Madam Hapney stuck to the wall and had to tell herself that Madam Hapney was gone. Inside was the vile witch—and only the witch. There was no saving Hapney. That was just a shell the high priestess had stolen.

"Fucking say *something*, you cunt!"

Melissa glanced behind her at the mutilated remains of all the Mushroom Cult girls she had just eradicated, then turned to face Anya. "I'm falling in love with the thrill of the kill …"

Anya tried to close her eyes so she wouldn't see what the girl planned to do with the three rows of fangs she saw in Melissa's mouth when she spoke, but the witch wasn't quick enough. The last thing she felt was what seemed like a million razor blades simultaneously ripping out her throat.

A burst of orange light flashed in the center of the small clearing, and Melissa fell from the sky and landed hard on the ground.

Her parents rushed over and crouched next to her.

"Are you okay? Where the hell did you go?" Travis machine-gunned more questions at his daughter without waiting for an answer.

Melissa lifted her head to look at everyone.

"Oh, my God!" Gwen yelled and reached for her daughter's face.

"I'm fine. It's not my blood." Mel looked down to survey her sweatshirt. The entire front was painted in crimson. Her neck, chin, lips, and teeth were surely covered in blood too. She panicked and reached into her mouth. She ran her index finger along her teeth to confirm only one row existed—and none were razor sharp. She sighed in relief.

Scarlet took a few steps with Hank toward Melissa. "Is it over?" he asked.

Melissa glanced at the triangle and single eyeball tattooed on her wrist. "I don't know, Uncle Hank. I hope so." She dropped her head back onto the ground and let all the pent-up fear and emotions pour out of her.

And she didn't think she'd ever stop weeping.

"Welcome back, Mr. Smith. Checking in?" the desk clerk asked, his jaw hanging by a single tendon.

Smith sighed and glanced down the hallway. "You know what? I thought I stopped having these weird blackouts decades ago."

"Blackouts? I don't follow. This is the Vertigo Motel. And I assure you, you are very real here."

"I'm not supposed to be here."

"No one is *supposed* to be at the Vertigo. You just are. I have a special room picked out for you."

Smith looked back at the man as the foyer lights behind him flickered in an unsteady pattern. "I'm afraid to ask."

The clerk handed him a key. "That room." He pointed to the first door on the left.

Smith accepted the key and took a deep breath. "Let's get this over with."

"Oh, there's no leaving this time. You're *dead* dead. You're here to stay."

"Good gravy," Smith mumbled and headed for the room. He put the key in the lock and opened the door. When he entered, he noticed a woman tied to the bed. A clock over the headboard was stuck on 11:18.

"So, what turns you on?" she asked.

Smith remained silent and closed the door behind him. "Of all the moments in my life, *this* one is my Hell?"

"You don't have to rape the willing," the woman said on autopilot.

"Yep. Just keep playing out the scene." He sat in the chair by the window and heard the cat meow loudly outside. "You see, doll? I was outside that window with that cat, watching Covington and you. *Enjoying* Covington and you." Smith glanced out the window and saw his own face, forty years younger, looking through the glass into the room. "There

I am. And this very moment started me down that slippery slope I could never escape from."

"Well then, shut up. I'll punch the clock, and you can fuck me until the blood scares you," she said robotically.

Smith stood from the chair and took a last glance at his younger self watching the perversion that was about to happen. "Candy. Your name is Candy."

Candy didn't acknowledge him; she remained stuck in the playback of events.

"Well, your real name isn't Candy." Smith reached into his pocket and magically found a fresh pack of Smolens. He lit a cigarette and inhaled deeply. "So, where do we go from here? Am I supposed to kill you to finish the scene, or am I stuck in a loop in here?" He squinted one eye as he took another drag.

Candy started moaning and writhing in pleasure on the bed.

Smith watched silently and stole another peek at his younger self now taking snapshots with his old Kodak camera.

Candy went from her Academy Award–winning moans of ecstasy to writhing in fear and pain.

"Here it comes. Get ready for it."

A gunshot went off, and Candy lay motionless on the bed, blood pooling around the sheet under her neck.

Smith held his Smolens between two fingers and wondered what would happen next. Would the scene start at the beginning on an endless loop for all eternity for him, or would it let him graduate to the next chapter of his atonement?

What did the Vertigo Motel have in store for him? Whatever its intentions, he knew this place was his end of the road, no being revived in the hospital room this time.

Smith startled at a knock on the door.

SALEM, MASSACHUSETTS; 1994

EPILOGUE

"Miss Smith? What's *this* book about?" Stephanie asked, surveying the odd front cover devoid of words.

Melissa looked over her shoulder at her kindergarten student while still wiping the names of the primary colors off the blackboard with an eraser; each swipe of the eraser just smeared the colored chalk and didn't remove it. The eraser fell from her hand, bounced off the chalk ledge, and hit the floor in a white dust plume as she froze in place. She spun and strode toward a group of her students milling about the short bookcase of learning-to-read books.

She snatched the maroon-colored, leather-bound book from Stephanie's little hands. "Where did you get this?" She realized her attempt at keeping her voice steady had failed.

"Right there, Miss Smith." Stephanie pointed to a gaping hole in the top row of books.

Melissa's hands shook as her fingers traced the triangle and the single eyeball embedded in the leather cover.

"Well, what's it about?" Stephanie asked.

Without breaking her stare at the long-forgotten book, Melissa swallowed hard. "Everybody, back to your tables!"

"*Aww*, but we haven't picked our books yet!" Tommy whined.

"Now!" she barked.

Her kindergarten class went wide-eyed and scurried to their assigned seats at the classroom tables.

"Please practice writing the numbers one through ten on your papers," she said, almost to herself, as she flipped open the book's yellowed pages. She scanned the familiar non-English words, and her heartrate accelerated.

"I have to go potty," one student said.

"Just … *wait* a second!" Melissa closed the book and snapped from her bewilderment, scanning the class. "I'm sorry, guys. Yes, we'll take a bathroom break. Everyone line up at the door."

Melissa still didn't move as her class of kindergarteners got into a single-file line at the door. She glanced at her wrist to check her tattoo that mirrored the design on the cover of the book in her hands. Something felt macabre about holding Anya's lost book in a room surrounded by poorly painted animals and brightly colored letters of the alphabet strung on a rope above a chalkboard. She spied the hole where Stephanie had found the book and wondered how long it had been there. She didn't remember seeing it yesterday afternoon when she had tidied the room after dismissal. But more important than how did it get there was *who* had put it there.

She tucked the book under her arm, strode to her desk, and stowed it in the bottom drawer. "Okay, class. Let's head on out!" She tried to interject some cheeriness into the panic of her voice.

The student at the front of the line opened the door, and Melissa followed her class down the hallway to the two small restrooms. Her thoughts swarmed as she stood, monitoring the bathroom break, without engaging any of the students—or really being in the *now*.

"Miss Smith?" Stephanie tugged on Melissa's sleeve. "We're all done and ready to go back now."

"*Huh?*" Melissa snapped back to reality, her eyes focusing on her students instead of the cloud she had just been lost inside. "Okay, great. Single-file line back to the room, everyone."

She fell in line behind the last student and watched them snake into the classroom. She closed the door behind her and waited for the students to take their spots at their tables. She sat at her desk and couldn't help but sense the power emanating from the book trapped in her bottom drawer. She wanted nothing more than to dismiss class for the day and to head home to her small apartment she shared with her fiancé to inspect the book.

Was it actually Anya's old book, sinisterly finding its way to the person who had destroyed its owner? Was it a new book, meant for her to keep, sent from the netherworld, since she had absorbed Baron's book ten years earlier? Was it someone else's book, trying to send her a message?

The classroom door opened, and every student stood in unison. "Good morning, Principal Berger," they all said.

Melissa quickly turned her head toward the door and also stood to greet her boss.

"Good morning, children," Principal Berger replied. "How are you today?"

"Very well, thank you. And how are you?" they all responded, all slightly off from each other so it sounded more like a garbled mess of squeaky voices.

"I am very well. You may be seated."

Melissa concentrated every ounce of her being to stop her body from trembling in front of her boss. She didn't realize she had been scratching her wrist tattoo with her fingernails until she felt the flesh go raw. "I-I'm fine, Principal Berger. I don't think I'm feeling well."

"Do you need to go home?"

"I'll be fine. Probably just something I ate for breakfast."

Principal Berger nodded, then manuevered around the tables. "Tell me, children, what does Miss Smith have you learning today?"

More than half the students spoke at the same time, creating a cacophony of answers that sounded like *alphabet, plus and minus, colors, science …*

Principal Berger had fully circumnavigated the room and stopped at the front, next to the desk. "Who would like me to read you all a book?"

Every kindergartener's hand raised and wagged in excitement.

Principal Berger scanned the tables. "You, Miss Stephanie. Why don't you pick a book, and we can all see if we can read it together?"

Stephanie pushed back her metal chair with a squeak and rushed to the bookcase. She quickly browsed the spines and slid out the ones without markings on the sides. She settled on a Little Golden Book and ran to hand it over.

Principal Berger studied the cover and glanced at Melissa with a wide grin and raised eyebrows. "What a delightful pick.

Hansel and Gretel." She redirected her attention to Stephanie. "This is one of my all-time favorites. Come, children. Gather 'round." She leaned against Melissa's desk and waited for the students to sit in a semicircle in front of her.

"Look!" Stephanie squealed. "That's a weird bird!"

Melissa's heart hammered as her gaze darted to the window.

"Cool!" another student yelled as the whole class rose and ran to the window.

Principal Berger folded her arms and smirked. "That's called a vulture, children. Very powerful animals. Wouldn't you say, Miss Smith?"

Melissa felt her breath hitch. "Yes, very powerful."

The black bird of prey tilted its head and focused on a specific student.

Principal Berger furrowed her brows and approached the window, curious.

The vulture pecked at the glass directly in front of that same child.

Melissa's back went rigid as she tried to see over the heads of her students at who the vulture was communicating with. She tried to figure out what the sudden appearance of the bird after ten years of absence signified—and on the same day a spell book, whose owner was unknown, mysteriously appeared. Had Anya clambered back from the chasm of nothingness to seek retaliation? Was Baron sending her messages from the beyond that everything was still copesetic and that a balance was still being maintained? Could this mean a new foe was building strength, who Mel would have to deal with? Was one of her students the next Chosen One ... but for whose benefit and purpose? Or was the bird just reminding her that they were never too far from her?

She watched her boss bend forward, stop inches from the glass, and make eye contact with the vulture.

Principal Berger slowly turned her head to acknowledge the child the vulture was fixated on. "These birds are powerful, child, but they are known to find very special and exceptional people."

Melissa startled when a kettle of vultures appeared simultaneously and beat their wings against the glass, much to the delight of the children. She closed her eyes and only hoped their visit would not be violent nor prove to be insidious.

Melissa Smith opened her eyes and screamed when the windowpane finally broke.

THE END

Golden Mirage CASINO

Poof & Snoofin BOUTIQUE

CPSIA information can be obtained
at www.ICGtesting.com
Printed in the USA
BVHW071059060821
612958BV00001B/7

9 781736 886717